"If you don't run away, I'm going to kiss you. And if I kiss you—"

"Who knows where that might lead," Brie finished for him. She went to move her feet and found she'd gone in the wrong direction. Toward him, rather than away. "Reed…"

He crushed her to him, claiming her mouth. She met him halfway, feeling like she could devour him. Hungry. So hungry.

"Starving," he agreed against her lips, before kissing her again.

Drowning in sensation, her knees buckled. His arousal, strong and fierce, pressed against her belly, where her simmering desire blazed into an all-consuming need. If he so much as asked, she'd rip off her clothes right there, right then, and climb on top of him.

As she contemplated doing just that, the bay window behind the couch exploded in a shower of glass.

Dear Reader,

What a glorious time of year—full of shopping, holiday cheer and endless opportunities to eat baked goods. For your shopping list I suggest this month's stellar lineup of Silhouette Intimate Moments books—romances with adrenaline.

New York Times bestselling author Maggie Shayne delights readers with *Feels Like Home* (#1395), an emotional tale from her miniseries THE OKLAHOMA ALL-GIRL BRANDS, in which a cop returns to his hometown and falls for a woman from his past. Will a deadly threat end their relationship? In Maggie Price's *Most Wanted Woman* (#1396), from her miniseries LINE OF DUTY, a police sergeant is intrigued by a bartender with a dark secret and an irresistible face. Don't miss it!

You'll love Karen Whiddon's next story, *Secrets of the Wolf* (#1397), from her spine-tingling miniseries THE PACK. Here, a determined heroine seeks answers about her past, which leads her to a handsome sheriff with his own secrets. Can she trust this mysterious man and the passion that consumes them? Michelle Celmer's story is *Out of Sight* (#1398), a thrilling tale in which an embittered FBI agent searches for a missing witness and finds her…in his bed. Will she flee before helping bring a killer to justice?

So, take a break from the nonstop festivities and get engrossed in these fabulous love stories. Happy reading!

Sincerely,

Patience Smith
Associate Senior Editor
Silhouette Intimate Moments

Please address questions and book requests to:
Silhouette Reader Service
U.S.: 3010 Walden Ave., P.O. Box 1325, Buffalo, NY 14269
Canadian: P.O. Box 609, Fort Erie, Ont. L2A 5X3

KAREN WHIDDON

Secrets of the Wolf

Silhouette®

INTIMATE MOMENTS™

Published by Silhouette Books

America's Publisher of Contemporary Romance

SILHOUETTE BOOKS

ISBN 0-373-27467-X

SECRETS OF THE WOLF

Books by Karen Whiddon

Intimate Moments

One Eye Open #1301
One Eye Closed #1365
Secrets of the Wolf #1397

Signature Select Collection

Beyond the Dark
  *"Soul of the Wolf"

*The Pack

KAREN WHIDDON

started weaving fanciful tales for her younger brothers at the age of eleven. Amidst first the Catskill Mountains of New York, then the Rocky Mountains of Colorado, she fueled her imagination with the natural beauty of the rugged peaks and spun stories of love that captivated her family's attention.

Karen now lives in north Texas, where she shares her life with her very own hero of a husband and three doting dogs. Also an entrepreneur, she divides her time between the business she started and writing the contemporary romantic suspense and paranormal romances that readers enjoy and that she now brings to Silhouette Intimate Moments. You can e-mail Karen at KWhiddon1@aol.com or write to her at P.O. Box 820807, Fort Worth, TX 76182. Fans of her writing can also check out her Web site at www.KarenWhiddon.com.

This one's for Floyd and Sarah and Lavenia and Dennis—family, yes—but friends, too.

Chapter 1

Lost! One more wrong turn and she'd probably end up in Massachusetts, which was so not where she needed to be. Pulling over to the side of the two-lane road, Brie Danzinger consulted her brand-spanking-new map of New York State, folded to reveal the Catskill region.

According to this, once she'd turned off Highway 17, she should only have had a few more miles of twisting, tree-lined road before she reached her hotel on the outskirts of Leaning Tree. A straight shot.

But apparently she'd turned one time too many. No surprise there. Back in Colorado, her dad had always joked she'd inherited a no-sense-of-direction gene from him at birth. The noticeable absence of street signs didn't help either.

Brie rolled down her window, inhaling the pine-scented air. There were no houses that she could see, no gas stations or convenience stores—nothing but trees, trees and more trees. Oaks and pines and maples battled with evergreens to spread branches toward the sun.

She sighed and attempted to refold the map back to the precise rectangle. Halfway through, she gave up and tossed the thing on the seat. The woods beckoned, tempting her with shifting shadows and moist earth. She might as well stretch her legs and walk off some of her frustration.

Slipping into the sheltering forest, she rolled her shoulders, feeling the tension lift, as though stolen away from her by the light breeze that ruffled the leaves. Somewhere nearby, a rabbit watched her—how Brie knew this, she couldn't say and didn't care to analyze. She simply knew.

From a branch high above, a squirrel chattered, scampering unafraid among the treetops. A crow cawed, and a blue jay screeched an answer. Brie smiled, pushing aside branches until she reached a small clearing. Transfixed by a shaft of sunlight that turned the foliage to emerald, she breathed in deeply, letting the scents and sounds of nature wash over her. She finally felt at home, oddly enough in a place she'd never been. Something resonated with her here in these woods, in tune with the steady beat of her heart and the rise and fall of her chest.

Peace.

Who knew? She'd traveled nearly two thousand miles to find her past, and fallen in love with a patch of forest.

"We shoot trespassers on sight around here."

Brie jumped and spun, swallowing back an instinctive scream. Her father's lifelong warnings rang in her ears. A silver-haired man glared at her, arms folded. An older man, his lined face wore an expression of shock. He seemed to have come out of nowhere; she hadn't heard even the slightest rustling of the leaves.

"I'm sorry?" Surely she hadn't heard him correctly. "What did you say?" She glanced around, unable to see her car or even the place where she'd entered the forest.

"You!" Recoiling, eyes widening, he spat at her. His voice quivered with what sounded like surprise and hope. "Elizabeth? What are you doing here? You're supposed to be dead, you hear me? *Dead.*"

Elizabeth had been her mother's name.

She took a step toward him, and then froze. "I—"

The emotion shining from his dark eyes made her pity him. Elizabeth Beswick had died over twenty years ago. Obviously, she still lived on in this man's memory.

"Liz, where have you been hiding?" His mouth worked. "Why did you stay away so long?"

"I'm not—"

"Elizabeth," he repeated, one hand stretched out clawlike toward her, his tone beseeching.

Geez. She took a deep breath. "I'm not her. Elizabeth was my mother's name. But she's dead." Suppressing the urge to comfort him, she swallowed. "I just got here, been driving for days. All the way from Colorado."

The man stopped, the expression on his face changing to confusion. He shook his shaggy head once, like a dog shaking water from its ears. The pity she'd been unable to keep from her voice must have reached him. Rooted in place, he continued to stare, the emotion in his eyes changing to anger.

"You're trespassing," he spat.

"Actually, I'm lost." She tried for a smile. He wasn't having any of it. In fact, his obvious embarrassment over mistaking her for a long-dead woman appeared to enrage him.

"I posted signs."

"I'm sorry, I didn't see them."

His eyes narrowed as he advanced on her.

Time to beat a retreat.

"I'm going to leave now." Speaking calmly, in a rational tone, Brie shifted her weight and began moving slowly backward, wincing as dead leaves shuffled under her feet. She'd make no sudden motions, nothing to alarm the now furious man or bring out the predator instinct in him.

Predator instinct? Where had that come from? Some melodramatic vein she hadn't known she possessed?

The greens and golds and shadows, no longer soothing, now felt menacing. Even the birds had gone silent. The absence of normal forest sounds told her more than anything her fear was not entirely unfounded.

"I'll be out of your way in a moment. My car is just over there." With a jerk of her chin she indicated the direction. If she cut her eyes, she could see her Mazda's bright red paint through the trees. A few more yards.

Foolish or not, she felt a full-fledged panic attack coming on. No! Not now. Somehow, she needed to control it. She needed to be able to think rationally.

He continued watching her, one corner of his lip curled in a snarl. Still, he made no threatening moves toward her, so she continued to back away slowly.

Five yards. Three. Breathing hard, she pressed the remote, unlocking her car. Giving in to her panic, she crossed the last two yards in a flat-out run. Fumbling with the handle, she yanked open the door and jumped in, relocking the vehicle. She took several deep breaths, tried to slow her racing heart, and cursed panic attacks in general. Her hands shook as she fumbled with the key and switched on the ignition. Slamming the gearshift into Drive, she cast one final look at the shadowy woods before peeling out.

The man hadn't followed her out of the trees. But he watched her still—she'd bet on it.

Once back on the road, she found she'd been too hasty earlier in thinking she was lost. As the map had promised, she drove two more curves in the road and she saw a sign proclaiming Leaning Tree City Limits. Half a mile more and she arrived at her motel.

Still battling the edge of panic, she managed to check in and make it to her room. Once there, Brie tossed her keys on the double bed and took a deep, shaky breath, trying to figure out what had just happened.

That man had mistaken her for her mother. Even worse, he'd acted as though he'd loved her or, at the very least, had some sort of relationship with her.

The sad, crazy man in the woods was bad enough. What horrified her even more was her reaction. Panic attacks again? No way. With the exception of the night she'd found her father, dead of a massive heart attack, she hadn't had a panic attack since she was seventeen. Why here? Why now?

Exhaustion made her stagger. She'd been driving nonstop for sixteen hours and she needed to rest. Yanking off her shoes, she sank onto the bed with a sigh. She'd try and get some sleep.

Tomorrow, her new life would begin.

Police Chief Reed Hunter nodded patiently as he took Eldon Brashear's report. Leaning on the front counter, he cursed the bad timing that had made Eldon drop by while the guys had taken Tammy, the receptionist, out to lunch for her birthday. Normally, taking this kind of report was her job. Hoping to catch up on paperwork, Reed had volunteered to man the office, even though he could have gone along and forwarded the phones to his cell.

So much for paperwork.

"I thought I was seeing a ghost." Eldon shook his head. "I'm telling you, you might have been only a boy when Elizabeth Beswick died, but this girl was her spitting image."

"You don't say," Reed repeated for the third time. Everyone knew Eldon had been enamored of the woman, long dead. Now the elderly man was seeing things. "Well, I'm sure it was just a weird coincidence. No doubt the trespasser drove on down the road."

"She claimed she was her daughter."

With a sigh, Reed wrote that information down. No one had seen hide nor hair of Elizabeth's husband, Tom—or their baby girl—in the twenty-odd years since her death.

Ignoring this, Eldon continued his invective against nosy outsiders with no respect for laws. "I had No Trespassing signs posted. She ignored them."

"Calm down," Reed interrupted, before Eldon got started again. "No harm, no foul. I'll file the report. If she shows up again, call me." He glanced at his watch. Tammy and his three deputies should be returning any moment. It was long past his own lunchtime and he was starving.

Still grumbling, Eldon finally took the hint and turned to go.

The bell over the front door jingled. Reed looked up, squinting as the bright sunlight reflected off the glass. A slender young woman with spiky blond hair came inside.

Reed looked up, met eyes the clear blue of a summer sky, and his gut tightened. He swallowed, momentarily unable to catch his breath.

Eldon swore. "You."

"You!" She gasped at the same time. Backing away, she stumbled, nearly tripping over the threshold.

"Wait." Reed regained enough equilibrium to use his best policeman's voice. Kind, yet authoritative. He couldn't seem to stop looking at her. Eldon was right—she did look achingly familiar. And beautiful. He inhaled again, wondering why she smelled like peaches. "Can I help you, miss?"

Her gaze locked on his and he felt it again, that sensation of something tugging at his gut. He wanted to reach out and trace her delicately carved features, to trail his fingers down the sensual curve of her neck, and revel in the softness of her smooth skin.

"Reed! That's her," Eldon growled, stabbing a finger in her direction. "She's the one I was telling you about. The trespasser."

Twin spots of color rose in the woman's pale cheeks. "Look." Lifting her chin, she took a step into the room. "I've already apologized. I was lost. I didn't realize I was trespassing on private property. I told you that. What else do you want me to do, pay for taking a walk on your land?"

Even her voice played on his insides. Reed shifted his weight and scratched the back of his neck, wondering why.

"I don't want your money." Eyes narrowed, Eldon

glared at her. Muttering under his breath, he stalked to
the exit. The bell jangled again as he jerked on the door.

"Chief, you deal with this," he tossed over his shoulder. "If she is Elizabeth's daughter, she's your problem
now, not mine. Just make sure she doesn't set foot on
my land again." The door slammed and Eldon was gone.
Leaving Reed alone, half-angry himself at the way this
staggeringly beautiful young woman affected him.

Her generous lips curved in a rueful smile. "Welcome
home, I guess."

"You *are* her." He spoke quietly, but with a dawning
sense of amazement. He let his gaze roam over her, ignoring his still-unsettling reaction. Wisps of golden hair
framed her heart-shaped face. She had an ethereal, yet
wild beauty, a sensual contrast of delicacy and strength.
Pack. He blinked, clearing his throat, and held out his
hand, aching to touch her in even this small way. "Welcome back. We've wondered when you'd come home."

Her eyes brightened as she took his hand. The instant
his fingers closed over hers, he felt a connection. Still
reeling from that, he narrowed his eyes, wondering.

She didn't appear to have noticed anything unusual.
"I like the sound of that," she mused. "Home."

A chill ran along his spine at her words. He needed
to speak, to say something, no matter how inane. "Brie
Beswick, back in Leaning Tree after all these years."

"Brie Danzinger, actually."

Belatedly he remembered Elizabeth's husband, Tom
Danzinger. Still, considering the Beswick's habit of re-
taining their maiden name, even after marriage, this
surprised him. Something must have shown in his expression, because she shook her head.

"I know all about the tradition of keeping the Beswick name. My father told me. He and my mother compromised by hyphenating the two names, but Beswick-Danzinger was such a mouthful, I dropped the Beswick part. Legally, that's still my name, but I've gone by Danzinger now for years. Made my father happy, too." She smiled faintly.

"How is your father these days?"

Her smile faded and a shadow darkened her blue eyes. "My dad died two months ago. That's why I'm finally here."

"I'm sorry to hear that." Had her father refused to let her visit Leaning Tree all these years? Why? She had family here, family who'd never stopped missing her, wondering how she was, worrying about who had acted as her Nya, initiating her into the secrets of the change.

"The entire town has wondered about you for decades." He still felt unsettled, a feeling he wasn't used to and didn't like. He took a deep breath, more to redirect himself, and inhaled the scent of peaches. Damn. "We all wondered why you never came back for a visit."

She leaned forward, her brows furrowed. "Until my dad died, I didn't even know this place existed. He never spoke of Leaning Tree, never told me I had family here. After he passed away, I honestly thought I was alone in the world."

No one in the Pack was ever truly alone. She should know that. A horrible thought occurred to him. What if she didn't know that either? What if sexy Brie Danzinger had no idea she was a shape-shifter?

Did she know the rest? What she was; what they all were? He searched her long-lashed eyes, noting the gray flecks mingled with the blue, a common sign of her heritage. Did she know her mother had been a shifter, able to change shape into a wolf? How could she not? Since the shifter gene was hereditary, and all halflings could shift, Brie Danzinger had to have been changing since childhood, hadn't she?

Again realizing he was staring, Reed cleared his throat. "You look like her," he said, uttering the first thing that came to mind. "I knew your mother well."

Reed'd had a crush on her mother, once. When he'd been a young cub, Elizabeth Beswick-Danzinger had been his Nya, mentoring him in controlling the change from human to wolf. Later that year, Elizabeth had been found dead, an apparent suicide. The entire town, or at least those who were Pack, had been shocked. As soon as the inquiry closed, Tom Danzinger had taken their toddler daughter and left town. That had been twenty-two years ago. Neither had been heard from since.

Until now. Now that daughter was grown. Lithe and gorgeous and, from the restless energy about her, a lot like her mother.

Brie stiffened, giving a small nod. "I barely remember her. Sometimes, I think I can smell her perfume, hear her voice, but then it's gone. I was only two when she died." She bit her lip. "All my life, my father was all the family I knew."

Her father. He'd been human, not Pack, but accepted because Elizabeth had loved him. But after Elizabeth's death, when he'd stolen the little halfling Brie away, most of the town had wanted to go looking for him, for Brie. Several had searched for months. Years. She was Pack, by right of birth, and they looked after their own.

Didn't she know that? Didn't she know any of it?

With another restless movement, she began to pace.

The confines of his small office didn't give her much room to maneuver, but still she blazed a trail around his desk.

He noted her long-legged stride with masculine approval, trying to decide how to best broach the question he most needed to know. Finally, he decided to just ask. Directness had always served him best. "Ms. Danzinger?"

"Brie," she corrected, automatically.

"All right, Brie then. Have you er, *changed*?"

"Changed?" Nothing but confusion showed in her face. "Since I was two? Sure I've changed. I'm twenty-four now. I've spent most of my life out West, in places like Lincoln, Nebraska, and Boulder, Colorado. What did you expect?"

Reed wanted to groan. She was Pack. A shape-shifter, born, but not raised, and she really had no idea of her potential, no idea at all. How was that possible? What had her father done? Hounds help him, if Tom Danzinger had appeared right now before him, Reed would have wrung the man's neck. The only way to keep her from changing into a wolf would be medication. Of course. "Do you have allergies?"

"What?" Now she regarded him as though *he* were crazy. "Allergies? Why?"

"Humor me. Are you taking any medications for allergies?"

She named a popular brand of allergy pill, now available over the counter. "What does that have to do with anything?"

He couldn't tell her the truth. She'd think he'd gone insane if he told her those particular pills suppressed the body's need to change shape. Instead he muttered some lame excuse about pollen and changed the subject. "How did you find out about Leaning Tree?"

"After my father died, I was going through his things. I found a box of pictures, some old letters, and learned I actually had family, people who might…" She swallowed, looking away. "Want to meet me."

He must have made a sound of protest, because she sighed. Her long lashes swooped down to cover her eyes. When she raised her gaze to his again, he felt it as if she'd touched him.

"Beswicks. Aunts and uncles, cousins. A whole slew of people I never knew about. Learning about them brought me joy in the middle of grief." She seemed to weigh her words carefully. "Though I'm not sure why, my dad always told me we only had each other. I never questioned him. We were together, a family. That was enough."

Reed wanted to swear out loud. What the hell had Tom been thinking? "What did Marilyn think about all this?"

Her blank look had him clenching his jaw. "My aunt?"

"Yes. Marilyn Beswick. You haven't met her?"

"Not yet. I only just got in."

"And came here first?"

She nodded. The lift of her chin dared him to ask her why.

He wasn't biting. "Well then, if you don't mind, I'd like to call your aunt and let her know you're here. She can start passing the word on to the rest of the Beswicks—and there are quite a few." He reached for the phone.

"No, please." Her hand on his arm stopped him. Again he felt her touch like a brand. "I'll do it myself, later."

His stomach growled, reminding him he'd yet to eat. A glance at the clock told him Tammy and the guys were long overdue to return. He decided he wasn't waiting any longer. "Have you had lunch?"

Still staring at him with those summer-sky eyes, she slowly shook her head. "No."

"Me neither." Running a hand through his hair, he felt restless, as though he needed to run a mile or two. Seizing on the excuse, he smiled. "Why don't we go get a bite to eat and then I'll take you around town and introduce you to your family. How's that sound?"

She cocked her head, considering. "Well, now that you mention it, I did skip breakfast." When she smiled, the effect was so dazzling that he had to remember to breathe. "I am pretty hungry. Yes, I'll have lunch with you. But no to the family. I still want to do that myself."

Headed for the door, Reed paused. "Oh? I thought that's why you came here first."

"No." Something in her face, desperation mingled with sorrow, stopped him. "That's not why I'm here to see you." Lush mouth set in a grim line, she swallowed, drawing his gaze to the graceful line of her throat. "I came to talk to you about my mother."

"Your mother?" He went blank for half a second, belatedly wondering if she knew the truth about that as well. The way her mother had died was no secret, but he wouldn't put it past her father to have somehow kept this from Brie as well.

Her next words confirmed his suspicion.

"I believe my mother was murdered. My father thought so, too, though he wouldn't talk much about it. I'm here because I want you to reopen the investigation into my mother's death."

Chapter 2

Hell hounds, could things get any worse? Hadn't her father told her the truth about one single thing? While Reed didn't want to hurt her, he couldn't allow her to fool herself, not about this. It was too important. Especially since she'd be meeting her family soon.

"Brie, I'm sorry." Keeping his gaze level, he slowly shook his head. "Your mother wasn't murdered. There was an investigation, twenty-two years ago when it happened. They concluded she died by her own hand. Suicide. No one here wanted to believe it either, but that's the way it happened."

Brie's eyes blazed azure. "I've seen the newspaper clippings—my father saved them. I know that's what all the reports say, what conclusions were drawn, but they're wrong."

Crossing the room to him, she leaned in close. "I

know you don't take me seriously, yet. But I have proof."

Inhaling her peach scent, he caught himself before he leaned in to meet her halfway. "Proof?"

"These." Opening her purse, she removed a packet of yellowed letters, rubber-banded together. "These are letters to my mother, from an anonymous man. My father said she kept them hidden from him. He didn't find them until it was too late, and she was dead. My mother had a stalker. Someone here in town."

"A stalker," he repeated.

"Yes. Officer…" she peered at his badge, "…Hunter, I think this stalker killed my mother. She wouldn't have committed suicide. She had too much to live for."

"Call me Reed," he said automatically. Years ago, he'd thought the same thing after learning of Elizabeth's death. So had most everyone else. But too much time had passed. He could hear the Pack Council—they wouldn't want to reopen old wounds. They'd say Brie Beswick—er, Danzinger—had come home with her "proof" twenty-two years too late.

Still, the idea of reopening the case, of clearing his Nya's name, was more seductive than he'd have believed possible.

He took a moment to consider. Did he really want to get into this? Reopen a case that had been put to bed a long time ago? The stack of paperwork on his desk told him clearly how many other things he had to do. In addition to serving as acting police chief, he traveled all over the county educating children on the danger of drugs in his role as DARE officer. He spoke at various Rotary and town functions, and taught part-time at the county law enforcement academy, training recruits. He worked enough twelve-hour days as it was, striving for acceptance. Did he really want to jeopardize all that?

He thought of Elizabeth Beswick's many kindnesses to him as a child, when others had treated him as an outcast, and realized he had no choice.

Decision made, he took a deep breath. As an officer of the law, he knew full well there was no statute of limitation on murder. Twenty-two years later, he'd give her daughter the benefit of the doubt and reopen the old files. Who knows, he might stumble across something other investigators had missed. Because he'd so admired Elizabeth Beswick, he'd always disbelieved the suicide finding. The vibrant, happy woman he'd known would never have taken her own life.

"I'll need to see the letters, of course."

Smiling, Brie held them out to him.

"Not now," he motioned them away. "Later." Yanking open the door, he stepped aside for Brie to pass.

She didn't budge. "Does that mean you'll reopen the case?"

He sighed. "After lunch."

Her smile spread, became a grin. Reed actually began to sweat.

"Thank you." She made a move, as though she might hug him, but stopped short. "Thank you," she said again, more softly.

Outside, the sound of car doors slamming told him the others had returned. He shepherded Brie toward the parking lot, lifting a hand at Rasinski and Saucier, who regarded him curiously. Tammy's mouth fell open, and Reed shook his head in warning. Now was not the time for questions.

* * *

Though Reed Hunter had promised to reopen the investigation into her mother's death, Brie still heard the doubt in his deep voice. The handsome police chief was probably only humoring her so he could get her out of his office and go eat his lunch.

Even now, her father's constant warnings rang in her ears. *Watch your back, stay alert, listen.* Even here—especially here—she knew she should be on her guard. Walking ahead of Reed, she refused to let her shoulders sag. She'd been living with fear her entire life. Conquered it, defeated it, again and again and again. Sometimes she felt like she'd been jumping at shadows since she could walk. No doubt the panic attacks were related to her father's paranoia.

Studying the police chief covertly, Brie wondered what kind of man he was. Tall, broad-shouldered, and classically handsome, he had an aloofness about him that reminded her of herself. He was…different. Like her. Scarred by whatever battles he'd fought in his own childhood. A kindred spirit.

She nearly laughed cynically at her musings. Realistically, Reed Hunter was one of the sexiest men she'd ever met. He moved like he was comfortable with his body, with the same unafraid awareness of his surroundings that a lion or tiger might have. As if maybe he hadn't always walked on the right side of the law. He looked out of place in his uniform.

Perversely, bad boys had always appealed to her, in spite of, or maybe because of, her fear.

They reached his vehicle, a new, navy, Chevy pickup, with the Leaning Tree Police Department insignia on the side.

"Wow," Brie said, impressed as she climbed inside. "I wouldn't have thought a small-town police department could afford something like this. This must have cost what, seventy-five, eighty thousand? Assuming you've got it outfitted properly."

Backing from his parking spot, he shot her a look, one dark brow raised.

She laughed. "Citizen's Police Academy. It's a twelve-week course. I learned all about what you guys do, including the cost of your equipment."

One corner of his mouth lifted in a smile. Hands on the wheel, Brie couldn't help but notice how strong his muscular arms looked. And his fingers—he had capable fingers. The kind of fingers that had her wondering what they'd feel like on her skin.

He shifted into Drive and pulled out onto the street. "This pickup is fully equipped, of course. Special suspension, engine, video camera, radar—we have it all. Leaning Tree might be small, but we have a decent budget for law enforcement. And, if I do say so myself, a damn good police department."

She nodded, dragging her gaze away from his hands to stare out the window at the tree-covered hills that rose above them on every side. "I like the looks of this place. Though the Catskill Mountains are not much more than rolling hills compared to the Rockies, I feel at home here. Like this is where I belong. It's so beautiful."

He glanced at her curiously. "How is Colorado? I've never been out West, so I have no idea. I would have thought it'd be the same. There are trees and mountains, right?"

She closed her eyes, seeing the craggy shape of the Flatirons, the fog-shrouded outline of Twin Sisters farther north. How could she describe the sometimes overwhelming freedom of so much space, the vastness of the clear, bright sky?

"It's brown," she said, never good with words. "We don't get a lot of rain there, so the grass turns brown quickly. In the foothills, where I lived, there are trees, but they're smaller, crooked and bent." Waving her hand, she indicated the towering oaks, pines and maples lining the road. "Not like these. Much less confining."

"I've never felt confined here."

"That's because you've never been out West. Some people," she gave a self-conscious chuckle, "find so much openness oppressive. They might call Montana 'Big Sky Country,' but to me Colorado has a similar feel, with its views of endless sky." Even up in the mountains, she'd often felt the weight of all that sky pressing down on her.

"I don't think I'd like it. I'd miss the forests here." Stopping for a red light, he turned to study her. She found the ruggedness of his masculine features, his high cheekbones and firm jaw, achingly beautiful to look at.

She swallowed, forcing her thoughts to remain on track. "I can see what you mean. The farther northeast I came, the more the sky seemed to shrink and grow more distant, more elusive. And it's so green! Everywhere I look, there are trees. Large trees, hardwoods towering over evergreens."

"Cluttering up the landscape, eh?"

She regarded him thoughtfully. "No. You might think I'd feel that way, but I don't. They don't seem as if they're hemming me in at all. Rather, I find them sheltering, as though they're protecting me."

Strange, different, but Brie liked it. She'd bet her mother had loved this country. Her father had never mentioned New York, or the Catskills, not even once. This had seemed odd until she'd found the box full of her mother's history, after his death, and realized he'd taken her away to save her from whoever had killed her mother.

"Entirely possible," Reed drawled, letting her know she must have spoken her thoughts out loud. Then she wondered, as Reed's half smile changed to a puzzled frown. He cleared his throat before continuing. "Though most people would tell you this is a small town and we don't have murders here."

"That's what they said in Boulder, too, before that little girl was killed." Now why had she brought that up? Every single law enforcement office she knew, both in Colorado and without, foamed at the mouth whenever that case was mentioned.

This cop merely smiled. "I said *most people*. I've already agreed to reopen the case, now haven't I?"

At her nod, his smile broadened.

"You mentioned you knew my mother."

"I did. You look like her, you know."

She started. "So I've heard. But you must have been young, right?"

"Seven. I was eight when she died."

While she debated on how to ask a virtual stranger to tell her more, he changed the subject.

"What would you like to eat?"

Eat. Right. Food. "Do you have a sushi bar?"

One muscle twitched in his cheek as he shook his head. "Thai?"

Again a negative answer.

She gave a half shrug, not really caring. "Okay, then what kind of restaurants do you have here?"

"Several great hamburger joints, an excellent rib place, a steakhouse, a French restaurant, Italian and a couple of sandwich shops."

"No hamburgers." She grimaced. "I made the mistake of stopping at some greasy spoon in Pennsylvania on the way here. I paid for it too. Italian sounds good."

Privately, she doubted she could eat. Already her stomach tumbled with nerves. Meeting newfound relatives was going to be tough, especially since she'd never even known she had them. She couldn't help but wonder if they would like her or want her hanging around their town.

"They'll like you," he said.

Brie stared at him in shock. "Did I say that out loud, too? I'm pretty sure I didn't."

Confusion flashed across his face before he gave her a slow nod. "You must have."

Damn. She rubbed the back of her neck. "I guess I'm losing it."

"Big changes are always stressful."

"Changes." Her attempt at a nonchalant smile felt weak. "I've sold everything I owned. All I have is my car and the clothes I packed. I want to start over, to make a home here. I want to—" *Belong.* She couldn't say that, not to this man. He'd never understand. Every movement he made showed how comfortable he was in his surroundings. No doubt he hadn't had the experience of changing schools nine times in twelve years. No matter how friendly Brie had been, no matter how many friends she'd made, she'd never truly fit in. Not when the others had been together all their lives and she never knew when her daddy would say it was time to move on. She'd always been the outsider, with only her fear for company.

Though now she understood her father's reasons, knew he'd believed keeping them moving would safeguard her from whoever had murdered her mother, hindsight couldn't erase how the unsettled existence had made her feel.

This time, no one could make her move again. Here, in Leaning Tree, N.Y., she wanted to stay. She wanted to put an end to her fear, to once and for all stop looking over her shoulder.

All she had to do was catch a killer.

The light turned green and Reed pulled forward. As they drove into downtown Leaning Tree, she looked out the window, wanting to savor every moment of her first view of her new hometown.

Main Street looked like everyone's dream of Hometown America. Fascinated, she studied the beautiful Victorian homes. Their pastel colors and ornate trim made them look edible. "Gingerbread houses!"

Reed grinned. "I used to think that when I was a kid."

As they moved farther into town, larger brick and elaborate stonework homes replaced the whimsical frame houses. Various shops, including a root beer stand complete with carhops on roller skates, lined both sides of the tree-lined street. The stone church looked ancient and quaint, with its old-fashioned steeple and belfry.

"There's the high school." Reed pointed, one hand draped loosely over the wheel. Leaning Tree High, a three-story, faded brick building that looked like it had been built in the early 1900s, sat squat and square at the corner of Main Street and 12th.

"Did you go there?" Curiosity and envy made Brie ask. She couldn't imagine the luxury of being able to attend one single high school with the same group of friends since kindergarten.

"Yep." He glanced at his watch. "It's late, so we should have totally avoided the lunch rush, such as it is here." He made a right turn into a parking lot. "Here we are."

The Italian restaurant was set in the corner of a brick strip shopping center. Five or six cars were parked out front.

Getting out of the car, Brie was suddenly struck with a feeling of panic, the same kind of turn-and-run compulsion she'd often had as a child starting a new school. Panic attack.

She gulped in warm air, willing her heartbeat to slow, gritting her teeth. "Reed?" Dammit, her voice shook. Taking a deep breath, she dragged her shaking hand through her hair. "Listen, I… I can't do this right now."

Staring, he stopped, no doubt wondering if he was dealing with a mentally unbalanced woman. She couldn't blame him.

"Can't do what?" He gestured at the wooden door. "Eat pasta?"

"I'm really not hungry," she lied, balancing on the balls of her feet so she could take off.

"Then have a cup of coffee while I eat. They have salads here too, you know."

"I'm sorry, but I think I'll pass." Unreasonable terror rose in her throat, making her gag. Any minute now, she'd start hyperventilating. She needed to get out of there before he saw.

Panic attacks were never pretty.

Chest tight, she fought the urge to run, to flee.

Reed's staring turned into cop alert. Outright suspicion. "Brie, Ms. Danzinger… Is everything all right?"

Shifting her weight from foot to foot, twisting her hands together to hide their trembling, she shook her head, unable to articulate. She took a deep breath and pushed back the roaring in her ears. She used to be a pro at mastering these things—damned if she'd let them take over her life again.

"Go ahead and eat." This time, despite her tenuous grip on control, only the barest quiver in her voice betrayed her. She took another deep breath. "I need to walk. Clear my thoughts."

"What about your car?" Frowning, he still looked puzzled. "It's back at the police station."

Heart racing, breathing ragged, she stepped away. Bounced back. Forced herself to settle. Summoned a smile from somewhere, lifted her chin. Breathe. Breathe. "I'll walk back to my car and head back to the motel."

He didn't seem convinced. In fact, from the stern set of his jaw she'd managed to turn on every instinct for trouble the man possessed. He was a cop, after all.

"Gotta go." Rocking onto the backs of her feet, she spun. Brisk walk, though she wanted to run. She lifted her arm in what she hoped was a friendly wave, and broke into a jog.

Damn.

Wishing for a cigarette even though she no longer smoked, clenching her muscles to control the tremors, resisting the urge to gulp air and moan, she took off and left Reed Hunter staring after her.

Only when she rounded the corner did she slow her pace to a brisk walk. Only when out of sight did she stop, hands on her knees, and give in to the waves of unreasonable panic.

For half a minute she stood, gasping for air, tears in her eyes. Then Brie stood, squared her shoulders, and lifted her chin. Determined to force the terror from her system, she began walking. The physical act of increasing her stride always helped.

Gradually she felt the tension leak away. She concentrated on her breathing, the steady rhythm of her feet slapping against the pavement, the regular pumping of her heart.

When she reached the actual town square, feeling relatively normal again, she made three trips around the circle before slowing to a stroll. As soon as she did, she began sneezing. Her allergies were acting up and she realized she'd forgotten to take her pill. She'd have to go back to the motel and get one, but first she wanted to eat. Now ravenous, she looked for a place where she could get a snack.

A few curious shopkeepers watched her. Finally locating a small newsstand, she went inside and purchased a bag of chips and a soft drink. With a friendly wave at the woman behind the counter, Brie headed toward the police department parking lot, where she'd left her car.

Once behind the wheel, she drove back to her motel. Forgetting to take her allergy medicine was totally unlike her. She'd put that down to her unsettled feeling. She'd go back to her room, stuff her face with chips, read a little and take a short nap. She wanted to be calm and composed when she met her new family. Maybe once she'd rested she could chase away the lingering remnants of panic and begin her new life.

Sheer bravado had carried her this far. No way was she chickening out now. Not when everything that mattered to her lay ahead. Though she realized finding her mother's killer wouldn't be easy, she had no choice. She wanted her future to stretch out before her with promise instead of terror, hope instead of fear.

On the way home from work, still thinking about the hauntingly beautiful Brie Danzinger and her unsettling effect on him, Reed pulled into Smokey Joe's. The parking lot was already two-thirds full. A bunch of the guys liked to hang out after work, eat ribs, have a beer and play a little pool. Though Reed usually stopped by on Friday nights and this was only Wednesday, he needed a distraction in a big way.

Brie. This afternoon, stark terror had shone from her gorgeous, blue eyes. While she'd tried to smile and act like nothing was wrong, the tremors that had wracked her slender frame had told him the truth.

She was terrified. But of what? Surely not of a hypothetical killer from twenty-plus years ago?

He sighed. He'd been reading her mind, a phenomenon shared only by those fated to become mates. Bad for him. Worse for her. He couldn't afford to think of any woman in those terms. Not ever again. Teresa had died because they'd become mates. No one deserved that fate.

That didn't erase the damnable truth. Brie Danzinger made him hunger for things he'd thought lost to him forever.

If he weren't police chief, he'd run as far away from her as he could. He'd fought long and hard to have this position. Spent years building friendships, gaining respect rather than animosity from the people of Leaning Tree. A son born into a cursed family didn't have it easy. But he'd overcome most of it—he growled, low in his throat. Most if it, save the loss of his beloved wife.

Still, despite the danger, his position alone meant he couldn't escape his responsibilities—to her deceased mother, his former Nya, and to Brie. The return of Elizabeth's daughter heralded trouble, on all fronts.

He parked the truck up front. Inside, country music blared over the loudspeakers. Joe's trademark peanut shells crunched underfoot. Reed often suspected folks ate the damn things just so they could toss them on the floor and wait for some poor drunk to slip and crash.

Taking a seat at the bar, he nodded at Rick Parks, two seats over to his left. Parks nodded back. Reed ordered a beer and Joe himself brought it, sliding the bottle across the counter into Reed's hands. A good judge of character, Joe didn't try to make small talk. He'd let Reed unwind first. Another reason why the place was so popular.

But when Reed took a pull on his beer, the first gulp slid down untasted. He rotated his neck and shoulders to relieve the tension. Keeping his hand wrapped around the sweating bottle, he swiveled in his seat and checked out the crowded room.

Three of the five pool tables were in use. Jared Ferndale and Miguel Ramos had one, playing silently, both intent and serious. They had a twice-weekly competition going on, third month running. Though Reed pretended not to know about it, rumor had it their pot was up to several thousand dollars now.

The other two tables were just guys having fun. Still in their gray and blue uniforms, most of them worked for the city. Sanitation workers and road maintenance guys were the most plentiful. Reed alternated between watching Tim Ruggeri's group and the other, thinking later he might join Tim's and sharpen his rusty skills.

A subtle shift in the atmosphere made Reed glance at the door. His heart skipped, then resumed beating.

Her. Brie Danzinger.

When she sauntered in, the roar died down to a more subdued murmur. Every guy was instantly aware of the new—and desirable—female in their midst. They were Pack, human sure, but also part wolf. That was their way. When they mated, they mated for life, but until they found the one, they had a hell of a good time testing the waters.

Reed's stomach clenched when her bright blue gaze found him. With a wave, she pushed her way through the crowd toward him. There was not a man in the place, married or otherwise, who didn't track her progress.

Great. Now they'd think she was claiming him, in the way of a Pack female. Only she wasn't Pack. Not yet. Not until she knew. Not until she changed.

"Hey." Without waiting for an invitation, she climbed up on the empty barstool next to him. Instantly solicitous, Joe took her order. Bud Light, Reed noted with reluctant approval. The same beer he drank.

"What are you doing here?" he asked. Though he tried to sound friendly, some of his irritation must have leaked into his voice, because she frowned.

"As you know, I skipped lunch, so I'm starving." She lifted one shoulder and sipped her beer. "I thought this looked like a good place to unwind. You?"

Blinking, it took Reed a minute to figure out she was asking why he was here. Since he'd changed out of his uniform, and was clearly not on duty, the question puzzled him.

"Same thing," he growled. "Ribs and beer." Now he sounded like the proverbial caveman, but maybe she'd leave him alone. He gripped his bottle and clenched his other hand in his lap to keep from touching her.

She didn't seem to notice. "Have you eaten yet?"

Draining the last of his beer, he regarded her warily. Finally, he shook his head. "No."

"Let me buy you dinner." She touched the back of his hand, sending a shock though him. "I owe you a meal after what happened at lunch today."

Half the room heard her invitation. Behind her, several in Ruggeri's group frowned. Despite his years of work, Reed was cursed and they all knew it. They eyed Brie, no doubt wondering if he'd told her. Scott Wells in particular, though he had to be old enough to be her father, watched her with stark hunger in his face. He sensed varying degrees of unease and anger radiating from the others.

Reed nearly groaned. Everyone in town would be all over him about this. He was probably the one single male, other than his uncle the priest, the women left alone.

"Reed?" she prompted. "Do you want to eat?"

He shook his head slowly, feeling like he was coming out of a fog. He was *working,* damn them. This wasn't a date. "Yeah. Sure. Dinner sounds good." He lifted his bottle to take another gulp of beer and realized it was empty. "Joe makes the best ribs in the entire state. The meat falls off the bone."

"Mmm." She licked her lips, the feminine gesture sending heat straight to his groin.

Hell hounds!

"Ready?" Her smile wavered slightly around the edges, as though she thought he'd pay her back for earlier and walk out on her.

He wasn't that petty. Taking her arm, he led her to a booth. He noted several people talking on their cell phones. By midnight, he figured most everyone in town would have heard of Elizabeth Beswick's prodigal daughter's fling with the cursed police chief.

Chapter 3

He was in for it now. He'd give it an hour, maybe less, before the calls would start coming in. He could only hope they'd be questions instead of accusations. Even once they learned the truth—that he was only acting in his capacity of law enforcement officer, they'd still take him to task, if they didn't string him up first. No one liked a cursed man trying to entice a woman into a relationship.

He thought of Teresa, and how hard they'd both worked to convince the townspeople that his family curse was only so much nonsense. The sad part of it all was that Reed had honestly believed his own words. Loving him, so had Teresa. He'd seen the censure mingled with fear in the older ones' eyes, though the younger people—those of his own age—had been more forgiving.

Until Teresa died.

Even at her funeral, the Pack had collectively blamed him. Once more, even though he was already police chief, he'd become shunned. Outcast. This time, he hadn't had Elizabeth Beswick around to help him, as she'd done when he was seven. Three years later, and he still felt if not for his contract, the council would let him go.

He'd worked damn hard to gain a small measure of respect. He'd have to walk a fine line between repaying the debt he owed Brie's mother and being careful not to cause any outrage.

His contract was up at the end of next month.

Swallowing, he pushed the thought away.

Joe brought over the menus and a second Bud Light for Reed. Brie opened her menu and began reading.

"There aren't a lot of choices," Reed warned, glad he sounded normal. "But everything is good. Even the salad." Joe had recently added salad to the menu for Lyssa, Alex Lupe's human, and vegetarian, wife. All of Leaning Tree was pretty much carnivorous, except for her.

When Joe returned to take their order, Brie asked for a full slab of ribs, causing Joe to grin in approval. Even though Reed could only eat that much meat when his body needed replenishing after changing into a wolf and back, he did the same. Once Joe bustled away, he leaned back in the booth and studied Elizabeth's daughter.

She took his breath away.

Steady, Hunter, steady.

Noticing his perusal, she smiled. "I can't wait to meet my family."

"You haven't met them yet? I thought you'd have gone by there this afternoon."

With a sheepish shrug, she grimaced. "I meant to. But driving out here exhausted me. I went back to the hotel and fell asleep. I only woke up an hour ago."

He tried not to think of how she'd look when she first woke, all tousle-haired and sleepy-eyed. "I still think it's odd that you came to the police station before going to meet them."

Her gaze skittered away. "I'm sort of nervous."

"Why?" He leaned forward, curbing the impulse that made him want to take her slender hand. "What are you worried about? This town has talked about the missing Brie Beswick ever since your father took off with you. Your family has wondered and worried and missed you. I'm sure your aunt is hurt that you haven't come by yet."

"She doesn't know I'm here. You're the only one who knows."

"Don't forget Eldon."

"The man in the woods?" She shuddered. "He didn't even believe me when I told him who I was. He thought I was my mother."

"And the Smiths who run your motel. You've never lived in a small town before, have you?"

"No." Her expression crumpled. "Damn. I hadn't thought of that. I'd planned on surprising her."

"Why don't we go by her place after dinner? I can take you to meet her, if you'd like." And that way, he could quash any rumors early. He was only doing his job, after all.

But Brie shook her head. "Not tonight. It's been a long day. I promise I'll go first thing in the morning."

"Good." He took a long drink of his beer, hating that he felt disappointed as well as relieved.

The group at the first pool table erupted in cheers.

Brie turned to look. While her attention was elsewhere, he took the opportunity to let his gaze roam over her. She had a slender, lithe beauty, graceful and willowy. Despite her apparent delicacy, he sensed she was strong, only due in part to her shifter blood. Her generous mouth would entice any man, even one who was not starving, and the curve of her waist made him long to sweep his hands over her shape. Merely thinking about this doubled his pulse, heating his blood like whiskey on a winter night.

Dangerous.

When she turned back to him, he felt a shock as her impossibly blue eyes met his. "About my mother's murder…I'm not going to mention anything to my aunt just yet. Or any of my relatives."

"Possible murder," he said automatically, glad of the distraction. Anything, to take his mind off the unsettling attraction she held for him.

An attraction he could never act on.

"Fine, possible murder. Still, have you thought about the possibility I'm right?"

He rolled his beer bottle between his palms while he deliberated. "I've thought about it, yes. I even dug out the old files, though I haven't had a chance to go through them yet."

"So you really are going to reopen the case. Thank you."

He shrugged, glaring past her at the group around the pool table who kept sneaking covert glances at them. Instantly, they turned away. "Truth is, her death has always bothered me. Your mother was a lovely, warm woman. Happily married, with a newborn daughter. Sure, your dad traveled a lot for his job, but he always came home.

Never cheated, that I know of. Both of them appeared single-minded in their absolute devotion to each other." As were all wolves, but he couldn't tell her that. Although her father had been human, not Pack. "There were none of the warning signs. No depression, no hints of drug use or alcoholism, nothing. Your mother truly had no motive for committing suicide."

"Then why…?"

"There was a note."

"So I've heard. Did you see it?"

He shook his head. "No. All that was before my time. I was only a kid then."

"But you're a cop now. Why didn't you reopen the case earlier?"

There were a hundred answers he could give. Glib answers, pointing out his small, overworked staff and numerous responsibilities. But the truth of the matter was, he'd had to be careful. By hiring him as a police officer, the council had shown a degree of acceptance. By promoting him to police chief, they'd given him back respect and trust. He hadn't wanted to jeopardize that.

He settled on the simplest explanation. "That case was old when I came to office. Old and settled. We had other things to work on."

She accepted his rationalization with a short nod. "May I review the files?"

"Sure. None of this is classified. It's all public record. You'll have to fill out a request, but that's it. The library also keeps the newspaper on microfiche. You might want to check that out, too."

She nodded. "I plan to start poking around tomorrow."

Their food arrived, heaping platters of meat and potato salad. They both dug in.

While he ate, Reed caught himself sneaking glances at her. With utter disregard for the sauce, she held her rib with both hands. He wondered if she realized she ripped at the meat with her teeth, like any good, red-blooded shifter.

They didn't speak again until they'd finished their meal. Declining Joe's offer of bread pudding, he stood, extending his hand to shake Brie's. Using his most professional voice, he bid her good-night. Though she looked slightly puzzled, she returned the handshake. Those watching appeared, to Reed's relief, to relax slightly.

He left her sitting alone in the booth, certain the moment he left, three or four of the guys who'd been watching her like sharks would descend. This shouldn't have bothered him, but it did.

He wanted her. Wanted her in the way a drowning man reaches for a life jacket.

He'd only met her that morning and he'd already been sharing her thoughts.

Trouble, that's what she was. Whether her mother had been murdered or not, Brie Beswick—no, Danzinger—was trouble.

Using the motel's cheap alarm clock, Brie rose before sunrise. Moving slowly in the predawn gray, she longed for a cup of good, strong coffee. The hot shower helped wake her some, but shortly before seven, she decided she'd get dressed and head across the motel parking lot to the small coffee shop.

As she locked the hotel room behind her, a crow cawed from a nearby tree. Brie glanced up at the sky. The sun glowed orange in the soft blue sky, providing a comfortable, early morning warmth that was nothing like the brisk chill of a summer Colorado morning. She could get used to this weather.

If only she could shake the unsettling sensation of feeling less and less at home in her own body.

Her heels clicked as she crossed the uneven pavement. She'd traded her normal jeans for black dress slacks and a sleeveless, deep purple cotton shirt.

Lost in her thoughts, she nearly missed the distinctive sound of footsteps behind her. *The sound of someone trying to move quietly.* Carefully, casually, she turned. And saw no one. There were several parked cars, but no one hid behind them. Not that she could see, anyway.

Nevertheless, she remained on alert. Living with her father had taught her well.

She listened hard, appearing not to. Nothing. Damn it. Still, she hadn't imagined the sound.

With a quick look over her shoulder, she increased her pace. Still no one. When she finally reached the restaurant and slipped inside, she rolled her shoulders to relax them and took a deep breath.

Focus on the positive.

The small place was bustling. Inhaling the odors of coffee and bacon and toast made her mouth water. Brie followed the hostess to a small booth. Unlike the rib place the night before, here no one paid her any mind.

She thought of the pleasant shock of running into Reed, of sharing a meal with him and realizing he, too, felt the attraction between them. She found it amusing that he had looked more at home in the smoky bar than he had at the police station.

Yet, despite the electricity that zinged between them

whenever they touched, he'd made no moves toward her. She'd checked his hand. No ring, so he wasn't married.

She ought to be glad. She didn't need a hot romance with the police chief of her new town. She didn't want anything to distract her from her focus—finding out who'd killed her mother and getting to know her new family.

Despite her resolve, she'd dreamed of him last night. Dreamed of wrapping herself around him, of making sultry, passionate love. Even thinking of these dreams in the bright light of morning made her feel warm and foolish.

Moving fast, the waitress brought Brie coffee, leaving the plastic carafe on the table. Brie ordered the largest breakfast available, something called the Meat-Eater's Special. The waitress gave her an approving smile as she noted the order and took off, though that might have been because this was the most expensive item on the menu.

The coffee carafe was empty by the time the food arrived. Three eggs, bacon, sausage and ham, plus hash browns and toast were piled on the oversized plate. Somehow Brie managed to eat nearly all of it, which amazed her. She'd never had a strong appetite before. She wondered why she did now.

After paying the check, she walked back to the hotel, keeping an eye out for a shadow. This time, she heard nothing, saw no one.

Once in her car, she took a deep breath and got out the directions to her aunt's house. Though they'd exchanged letters and a couple of phone calls, Brie felt awkward, like she was a new kid once again on yet another first day of school. Her aunt Marilyn lived across town. Hoping she didn't get lost, Brie drove slowly, seeing the stately homes alongside the tree-lined streets, but unable to appreciate them. Her nerves once again jangled and the filling breakfast she'd eaten now threatened to come back up.

Miracle of miracles, she didn't get lost. There was a first time for everything. Turning down Sowell Lane, she parked in front of a sturdy, brick bungalow and killed the engine. She stared at the house.

Her aunt Marilyn was inside. Her new life awaited.

Heart pounding, Brie got out of her car.

Flowers lined the pretty brick sidewalk. All her favorites, peonies and tiger lilies and zinnias, blooming in an explosion of tangerine and lemon and rust. The towering trees provided ample shade and the grassy yard was well maintained.

Climbing the brick steps, Brie wiped her palms on the front of her slacks, took a deep breath, and lifted her hand to knock. The front door swung open before her knuckles touched the wood.

A tall, heavyset woman with a shock of orange hair yelped in surprise. "There you are! Let me look at you! I swear I was just on my way over to that motel to see what was keeping you. Now here you are!" Her ample chest heaved, then she held out her arms. "Come here, child."

Aunt Marilyn. Throat aching, Brie couldn't speak. She could only jerk her head in a short nod and step into her aunt's plump arms.

Enveloped in a gardenia-scented hug, Brie sighed, throat tight. Her aunt chuckled, her large body shaking. "Welcome, welcome, welcome! We're so glad to have you back home."

Home. Despite Brie's fierce promise to herself earlier, her eyes filled with tears.

She clenched her teeth. She wouldn't cry. Wouldn't.

So of course she began to sob like a heartbroken child.

"Oh, sweetheart. You're here now, everything will be all right. We've missed you so, honey. Come on in." Smiling through her own tears, Marilyn kept her arm around Brie's shoulders and led her inside. Passing through a cozy, cluttered parlor, they went straight to the sunny, yellow-painted kitchen.

"The heart of my house." Beaming, the older woman went to a gleaming, old-fashioned refrigerator. "Would you like something to drink? I made fresh lemonade, and iced tea. Plus, there's cola, milk, juice, whatever you want."

"Lemonade will be great."

Pouring them both a tall glass, her aunt studied her intently. "You look so much like my sister, it's uncanny. I can't see Tom in you at all."

Brie nodded. "So he often said."

"You must miss him something awful."

"I do. My dad was a great father. I loved him very much."

"Of course you did. My husband—your uncle Albert—and Tom were great friends. He had to work today, but he's looking forward to meeting you. Brie Beswick, home at last."

"Danzinger," Brie corrected.

Marilyn frowned. "But...our family tradition..." Then, apparently seeing something in Brie's face, she waved her hand. "Never mind all that. I'm so glad to have you here. Of course you'll stay with us."

"I've got a room at the Forestwood Motel."

"Had a room." Beaming, her aunt squeezed her hand. "You don't need it any longer. As soon as I learned you were coming, I started preparing the guest room. I want you to stay here."

This small kindness made Brie's eyes tear again. "I guess I can…"

"Don't sound so uncertain. We're family, dear."

"Family," Brie repeated. "I can hardly believe all this. When my father died, I was shocked when I found out I had an entire family I'd never known about."

"So you traveled across the country to visit us." Marilyn laughed. "I'm so very glad you did. How long do you plan to stay?"

"I'm thinking of forever. I thought I'd look at houses, see what's available for purchase. There's nothing for me in Colorado anymore." She held her breath, waiting for her aunt to comment.

Instead, the older woman merely nodded. "You must have been lonely, child."

"Lonely?" Brie felt disloyal to her father's memory admitting it out loud, but she had been. "I had my father. We had each other." But she couldn't help thinking of what she'd missed, all the holidays bustling with family gatherings, the cousins, the aunts and uncles clustered around the Christmas tree, the food, the laughter, the love.

Her father must have believed the danger was great to have denied her all this.

Marilyn pushed herself up from her chair and squeezed Brie's shoulder. "You've got a lot of catching up to do, sweety. I've got photo albums. Pictures of your parents' wedding. Your mother and me as children. Would you like to see them?"

"Yes, I would." She took a deep breath. "I remember very little about my mother. After I leave here, I'm planning to go visit her grave. I've never seen it."

Her aunt froze. "Oh, you poor dear. Would you like me to go with you?"

Brie shook her head. "I think the first time, I'd like to go alone. But I was hoping you could tell me how to find it. I get lost easily. I understand she's not buried in the cemetery at the church."

"No." Mouth twisting, bitterness flashed across Marilyn's face. "The church doesn't allow suicides to be buried on hallowed ground, so she's not in the family plot. She's out at another cemetery, near the old quarry on the south end of town. It's not hard to find."

Most of the day gone, carrying a basket of flowers picked from her aunt's garden, Brie waved goodbye. In addition to the lemonade, she'd had tuna salad sandwiches for lunch, followed by cake and coffee, with the end result she now felt as though she needed to take a nap. She'd promised to return the next day, suitcases in hand, after checking out of her motel.

Her aunt was already on the phone, organizing a picnic the following weekend that she'd enthusiastically promised would be the get-together of the year.

Following Aunt Marilyn's directions, Brie managed to locate the tiny cemetery without difficulty. Things were looking up in the not getting lost department.

She got out of the car and stared at the final resting place of the mother she'd never really known. Deserted and peaceful, the iron-fenced square appeared to be no more than two acres, surrounded by forest on three sides. A small stone building—chapel or mortuary—sat on the other. The place had a well-tended air, with a freshly mowed, green lawn and orderly tombstones.

Opening the well-oiled gate, Brie went to the far north corner, toward the tallest oak tree. There, her aunt had told her she'd find her mother's grave.

Elizabeth Beswick. Beloved wife and mother. Brie gazed at the polished granite, noting the dates and the beautiful, stylized wolf carving decorating the headstone. Her eyes filled with tears.

"I'll find out the truth, mama," she whispered, echoing the promise she'd made to herself. "So you can rest in peace."

She laid the flowers in front of the tombstone. Then, chest tight, she wiped at her eyes and turned to go. When she reached her car, she noticed someone had tucked a flyer under her wipers. Snatching the paper off the windshield, she got in the car, unfolded it and began to read.

What? A chill ran through her. This was no advertisement. She read it again.

Typed on an old typewriter, it was a personal letter, praising her beauty, her kindness, her intelligence. Unsigned, the writer concluded with a promise to make personal contact soon. The latter sounded more like a threat than an invitation.

This was eerily similar to the first of the dated notes her mother had received. In tone, in language, right down to the typeface, with the faint letter *e*.

She carefully folded the note back in its original rectangle and tossed it on the floor of her car. This proved her mother's killer was still in Leaning Tree. Even more unsettling, this note proved Brie herself was now a target. As she'd intended, by coming here.

Draw the murderer out, then expose him. Even if she had to put herself in danger.

Her father's worst fears, come true.

Suppressing a shudder of revulsion, Brie started her car. She'd take this note to the police station and show the police chief. Even though he wasn't privy to her plans, Reed Hunter could help her decide what course of action to take next.

Dusk was settling as she pulled into the parking lot. She parked under a light, as her father had always insisted, and locked her car. Walking into the well-lit police station, Brie noted how the place actually felt comforting rather than sterile, unlike most other law enforcement buildings. Maybe because of the bright yellow walls or the heavy oak furniture, polished to a high shine, that filled the rooms instead of standard issue metal desks and chairs. The floor, too, was made of worn oak. No institutionalized linoleum for the Leaning Tree PD.

She'd noticed none of these things yesterday, which said much about her state of mind. And naturally, running into that awful man had distracted her. Today, there was a dark-haired woman seated behind the front counter. Two officers looked up from paperwork as she approached. She saw no sign of Reed.

The woman, whose name tag read Tammy, regarded her steadily. "Can I help you?"

Brie placed her hands on the counter, palms down. "I need to talk to Reed."

"Police Chief Hunter? Do you have an appointment?"

One of the officers stood. "Can I help you, ma'am?"

"No, thank you." With a smile to take the sting off

her refusal, Brie glanced around, hoping he'd magically appear. No such luck. "I'm afraid I need him. I don't have an appointment, do I need one?"

Before Tammy could answer, Reed strode into the room. Immediately, the temperature rose two degrees.

When he saw her, he froze.

"Hey," Brie said. "I need to talk to you."

Running a hand through his hair, he glanced at his watch. "I only have a few minutes."

"That'll be enough."

The receptionist glanced from him to Brie and back again. "You two know each other?"

Brie nodded. "I'm Brie Danzinger."

Tammy's mouth fell open. Then, recovering, she glanced at the other two officers, who were staring.

Reed motioned Brie to his office. Once she'd entered, he closed the door.

She had a sudden, immediate fantasy of catching his face, drawing his mouth to hers for a kiss. Whoa. Where on earth had that come from?

His chair creaked as he dropped into it. "Are you here to look through the files? I've set them up in the conference room, as I promised."

"Yes, but there's something else." Brie handed him the note. "Someone put that on my windshield while I was at the cemetery."

A line appeared between his eyes as he read. "It sounds like fan mail."

"It also reads exactly like some of the first notes my mother received, right down to the typeface. This was done on a typewriter, not a computer. Not too many people use those anymore."

"You mentioned those old notes of your mother's

yesterday. I need to see them. I'd like to photocopy them. And this." Pushing himself out of his chair, he left the room, returning a moment later with two papers. "Here you go." He handed a copy of the note back, watching as she carefully folded and slipped it in her purse. Then he placed the original in a manila folder.

"Would you mind showing me the others?"

"Of course not." At least he was taking this seriously. "I have the box in the backseat of my car."

He followed Brie outside.

Darkness had fully fallen. As she walked to her car, Brie realized the light she'd parked under had gone out. Or been shot out. Glass crunched under foot.

Reed grabbed her arm. "Wait."

But she'd seen her car. The same person who'd taken out the light had also smashed her passenger side window. Her front seat was full of glass.

"I don't believe this." Unlocking the door, she checked out the rest of her interior. "My CDs are gone, my map, and of course the money I kept in the console." As she peered into the backseat, she made a low sound of rage. "They took the box, too."

Eyes narrowed, Reed looked from her to the broken window. "Takes balls to do this in the police station parking lot."

"Yes." She couldn't keep the accusation from her voice. "But what I want to know is, how'd they know enough about the box to take it?"

"Brie, this looks like a random theft. Grab and run. They took anything that looked like it might be worth something." Moving past her to her car, he knelt down and did an extremely odd thing. Putting his face near the asphalt, he sniffed the ground. Then, muttering under his breath, he pushed himself to his feet, and turned a slow circle, doing the same thing to the air. As if he thought he could somehow detect the intruder's scent.

Brie stared, trying not to let her mouth hang open. Was the entire town this weird?

Chapter 4

While he used his most powerful sense to search for any lingering scent, Reed kept an eye on Brie. She eyed him like he was a circus act. If he'd thought he might be able to stir up some hint of recognition in her, he'd been wrong. He saw nothing but shock in her eyes.

Just like he smelled nothing but the scent of peaches.

"Come on inside." Brie didn't resist when he placed his hand on the small of her back and guided her back through the door. "We'll need to write up a report."

Tammy was leaving for the day. She regarded them curiously, but asked no questions. Instead, she handed Reed a clipboard and sheet of paper. "Greg and Peter are out on patrol. Sheryl Grabel is on dispatch."

He nodded, accepting the clipboard. "Have a nice night."

Mouth grim, she glanced at Brie before meeting his

eyes. "I'd say the same back, but I don't think so." She sailed out the door, head held high.

Reed sighed. A beautiful woman walks in and even his own people thought the worst of him. Glancing at Brie, he supposed he couldn't blame them.

"This will only take a minute," he told her, speaking of the report.

She nodded, sitting dispiritedly while he entered the details into his computer. Once he'd printed the report and given it to her to sign, she stood and leaned over his desk.

"I'd like to take a look at those files."

Glad she had no way of knowing how her closeness made his heart rate double, he glanced at his watch. Nearly nine. Though he rarely got out of here so early, his day officially ended at five. He was tired and hungry and wanted to go home and change clothes.

One look at Brie's expectant face decided him. "Sure. We can review them together. It's been a long time since they were made. With the objectivity of time on our side, maybe we'll find something the other investigators missed."

In the conference room, he'd stacked the files on the middle of the long table. He gave Brie two and kept two for himself. Taking chairs across from each other, they fell into silence as they both read.

About a half hour later, Brie closed her folder with a snap. Yawning, she stood and stretched. A stab of pure lust went through him. He longed to touch the pale curve of her skin where her shirt separated from her slacks.

Stupid.

"All finished?"

She nodded.

"So am I."

"Let's trade." She slid her folders across the table to him. "Mine had no mention of a stalker, or of her receiving any letters."

"I don't think she reported them."

"That, I don't understand." She shifted her weight from foot to foot. "It makes no sense."

"I know." Reed tapped the papers stacked neatly before him. "Reading through this confirms what I already knew. For all intents and purposes, nothing out of the ordinary occurred in her life. Your father traveled for his job, but he always came home. She had a lot of friends and family here, and spent most of her time with them. Plus she had you."

"Yeah." Glum-voiced, Brie shook her head. "Though these reports seem clear-cut and straightforward, her killing herself makes no sense. Didn't anyone question it?"

"Sure they did. No one in town wanted to think she would do such a thing."

"But they didn't have any suspects, did they?"

He looked at her, not wanting to be the one to tell her, but knowing she'd find out sooner or later. "A lot of people suspected your father had something to do with her death. Especially when he took off with you so soon after it happened."

She gasped. "No way. Not in a million years."

He held up a hand. "They didn't think he killed her. More like maybe they were having problems, and that drove her to end her own life."

"That's—"

"Hey, I'm not saying I believe it. I'm just telling you what people thought at the time."

She dropped back into her chair, leaning her elbows on the table. "Maybe that's why they didn't even look for a suspect."

He wanted to grab her and kiss her senseless. Of course, he did not.

"Brie, they had no evidence. No reason to think her death was anything other than what it seemed, a suicide. They might have gossiped about your father— you know how people are. But no one had proof of any kind of foul deed. You read the reports." Clenching his jaw, he tapped the paper again. "All signs led to suicide."

"You mentioned she left a note, but I haven't seen it."

"I haven't seen it either, though the report mentions it. There's one more folder we haven't looked through. Maybe it's in there."

Digging through the papers in the last folder, Reed located a plastic bag containing a slip of paper. "This must be it."

Eyes bright, she watched him. "Open it up and read it."

He did. "Hell hounds, you're not going to believe this."

"Let me see it."

He slid the paper over to her, watching while she picked it up and read.

"Same typewriter." She looked up at him, her eyes shining with excitement. "This matches the other notes my mother, and now I, got. The letter *e* is even faint. Has to be the same one." She combed a hand through her spiky hair, making it stand on end.

"You know what that means?" He crossed his arms.

"I do." If he expected to find fear, she wasn't showing any. "The same guy who was after my mother is now targeting me."

She didn't say what they both knew. As police chief, Reed's job was now clear-cut. If indeed Elizabeth Beswick had been killed, he had to make sure her daughter didn't suffer the same fate.

"He didn't threaten you." Reed felt obligated to point out the obvious.

"He didn't threaten my mother either, not at first." She made a face. "If those notes hadn't been stolen, I could show you." Examining the yellowed paper once more, she pushed back her chair so hard it fell over backward, clattering to the floor. "Oh my God."

"What?"

"There's no signature. My mother didn't sign this. Her killer wrote a fake suicide note!" Her voice rose. "I can't believe the police didn't question this."

He wondered about that also. "Maybe everything seemed so clear-cut to them. They had no reason to consider foul play."

"No reason? What about the notes the stalker wrote?"

"The suicide note is the only thing they had. Remember, no one knew about the letters she'd received."

Dully, she stared at him. "My father knew. He had them. Why didn't he say something?"

An urge to take her in his arms and hold her possessed him. He clenched his teeth until it passed. "Brie, he may not have found them until much later, maybe even after he was halfway across the country. He was grief-stricken and on the run. We'll never know."

Finally, she gave a reluctant nod, passing the note back. "I guess not. But I don't understand why she didn't tell anyone before…"

"From what you say, the letters started out nice. In those days people didn't talk as much about stalkers and serial killers like they do now. Especially here. Maybe she didn't realize the extent of the danger."

Brie pounced on his words like a cat after catnip. "So you agree with me. You think she was murdered."

"I…" He spread his hands. "I said it's possible. I've reopened the investigation, but we can't jump to conclusions just yet. We need more evidence."

"Someone in this town killed her." She lifted her chin. "Killed her and set it up to make it look like suicide. They even wrote the suicide note."

"Brie…"

She continued as if he hadn't spoken. "Look at the facts. She had a stalker, whose letters got increasingly more unbalanced and threatening. You can guess what happened next. She rebuffed the guy and he snapped. Decided if he couldn't have her, no one could. You see it all the time on the news and in movies."

"This isn't a movie. This is Leaning Tree. There's never been a murder here."

"That you know of," she shot back.

He crossed his arms. "Brie—"

"You're missing the point. It's going to get worse before it gets better. Don't you understand? I show up in town, looking exactly like my mother. Whoever killed her must have seen me, and knows what I have could harm him."

"Then you'll have to be very, very careful."

"Or…" Her wolfish grin made his chest ache. "I could be bait. Draw him in."

"That's a bad idea."

"Is it?" she challenged. "I think it's perfect. The guy is after me anyway—he's already written the first note. Why not use him, turn the tables on him for once?"

"Bad idea. You're not trained."

"So? You said you'd help me. Teach me what I need to know."

"I can't. There's not enough time."

"Fine." She shrugged. "I'll figure something out."

He nearly groaned out loud. Part of him admired her gutsiness, the other part wanted to haul her up against him and kiss some sense into her.

"Brie, I want you to promise me you won't try to do this on your own."

"I won't be on my own if you help me."

They locked gazes. Finally, to buy time, he nodded. Meanwhile, he wondered how he'd possibly justify assigning her round-the-clock police protection on nothing more than what looked like a fan letter.

"Let me do the investigating. You relax and enjoy your new family."

Shaking her head, she grimaced. "Right. I want to find this guy. Again, will you help me?"

"Of course I will. I'm the police chief." He led her out into the hall, toward the front door. "Although I want you to be careful, don't let this person ruin your homecoming."

Directly meeting his gaze, she lifted her chin. "I'll try not to. You know, I keep thinking of that Eldon Brashear. You need to investigate him."

"Eldon wouldn't hurt a flea."

"He threatened to shoot me."

"He's all bluster. He's just a lonely old man."

"A dangerous lonely old man."

Reed laughed. "Eldon's not a threat. I've known the man since I was a kid."

"At least see if he has an old, manual typewriter."

"That I can do."

His response seemed to satisfy her. Still, he moved sideways, careful not to touch her. She was standing too close. He could all but taste the peach-scented lotion on her skin.

Oblivious, she gazed up at him. "You know, by breaking into my car, it's like an open declaration of war."

"What?" He managed a strangled laugh. "You're being melodramatic. We don't even know for sure it was the same person. That might have been some punk kid."

She rolled her eyes. "And I think you're missing the point. This stalker isn't going to go away. Not if he's the same one who killed my mother."

He feared she was right.

The urge to change rose in him, pulsing through his blood. He'd been working so hard at blocking his desire for Brie, he'd channeled it into this—the need to become a wolf. He had to get Brie out of here. The last thing he wanted to do was frighten her.

She seemed loath to leave. "Did you know my aunt's organizing a big cookout this weekend, so I can meet the rest of the family?"

Focusing on her, he forced a smile. "So I've heard. She already called and invited me."

"Did she really?" She looked mildly embarrassed. "I wonder why?"

"This is a small town. Marilyn's invited just about everyone."

She titled her head, exposing her creamy white throat. "Are you coming?"

When he could speak again, his voice came out a growl. "I'll be there. In case your admirer shows up."

* * *

The next morning, Brie checked out of the motel and, bulky suitcases in tow, arrived at Aunt Marilyn's. In anticipation of her arrival, her aunt had prepared a huge breakfast, which rivaled the Meat-Eater's Special for size.

Her aunt took her suitcases over her protests and, one in each hand, bustled off to place them in Brie's new room. When she returned, she led Brie into the kitchen.

A balding, angular man sat hunched over his heaping plate. Marilyn beamed at him in obvious delight. "Albert! This is Elizabeth and Tom's daughter, Brie. Brie, your uncle Albert."

Pushing back his chair, he hugged her. He smelled of pipe smoke and sausage. His smile was as reserved as his wife's was broad. "You look just like your mother."

"Thank you." Brie laughed, nervousness bubbling up in her.

He kissed Marilyn on the cheek and went back to his breakfast.

Brie ate until she could hold no more. "I'm going to have to start working out if I keep eating like this."

Marilyn patted her round stomach. "Or you'll end up looking like me. Maybe I should consider joining a health club. There's a new one that just opened up in town."

Albert waggled his brows at Brie. "She'll never do that," he confided. "Marilyn knows I think she's beautiful just the way she is." Kissing his wife's plump cheek, he wandered off, chomping his pipe stem between his teeth.

After they'd cleaned the dishes, Marilyn showed Brie around the house.

"There's only one room that's off-limits." Her aunt indicated a closed door. "That's my private library. I'm the only one with a key to that room. Anywhere else in the house, feel free to roam. Make yourself at home."

The backyard looked like something out of a magazine, with vibrant flowers everywhere and the lush, emerald grass. Brie saw a rope hammock strung between two maples and knew she'd found a slice of heaven.

Uncle Albert left for work and her aunt left for her charity work at the animal shelter. And Brie unpacked her clothes in her gray and cream bedroom, feeling safer than she'd felt in years.

The morning of the picnic, Brie woke with familiar butterflies pummeling her stomach. Her aunt and uncle had gone ahead to help get things set up. As guest of honor, Brie didn't have to be there until later.

Fears. No. She refused to acknowledge them. She had no reason to be afraid. These people were her family now.

Brie dressed carefully, even though the gathering was casual. She tugged on her favorite pair of khakis, so well worn that the cloth felt as soft as a beloved T-shirt, and topped them with a coffee-colored, stretchy, sleeveless pullover. Low-heeled sandals completed the outfit. For ultracasual Boulder, she was positively overdressed. For Leaning Tree, N.Y., she suspected the clothes would be just right.

The butterflies in her stomach tumbled again. She pressed her hand to her midriff and shook her head, making her dangly earrings swing. Lifting her chin, she smiled at herself in the mirror. She fluffed her short hair and then ran a tube of clear lip gloss over her lips. Finally, she pronounced herself ready.

For the third time, she glanced at her watch. She'd gotten ready way too early. The picnic didn't even start for an hour.

Not knowing what else to do, she began to pace her room. She'd much rather walk in the woods, had been longing to in fact, but after the encounter with Eldon Brashear, she wasn't sure where this would be allowed. God forbid she accidentally trespass on someone else's property. Pacing indoors wasn't the same—no way she could work off her nervous energy.

Finally, she judged it time to leave.

Once in her car, she read over the directions Aunt Marilyn had provided and drove off. Ten minutes later, pulling up to a stop sign, she consulted the map again.

She couldn't find the park. Aunt Marilyn had said it was near the high school, but Brie had driven around that building twice now and hadn't found any sign of a city park.

With a sigh, she scanned the directions again. They really seemed quite simple.

Suddenly she heard the high-pitched squeal of brakes locking on asphalt. A beat-up old truck loomed in her rearview mirror seconds before it slammed into her.

The impact pushed her forward, causing her seat belt to cut into her chest and shoulder, throwing her back against the seat. Her sunglasses went flying. Her neck popped. She groaned. Even breathing hurt. She'd have bruises later.

Dazed, she unbuckled her seat belt and opened her door. Blinking to clear her double vision, she staggered around her car, steadying herself by holding on to the side while she waited for the other driver to emerge. He did not.

What if he'd been seriously injured? Smoke or steam

poured from under his crumpled hood. The radiator? Or worse? She approached the vehicle cautiously. The crushed bumper tilted at a precarious angle, hanging on by a single screw. From the look of the rusted metal and peeling paint, only a miracle had kept the old truck from utterly collapsing in a heap of parts upon impact.

A person was outlined through the cracked and dirty windshield. When he moved, she blew her breath out in relief. At least he wasn't dead.

As she approached, he saw her and started cursing. When Brie realized who had hit her, she nearly swore, herself.

Eldon Brashear.

Chapter 5

As she stepped back, Reed's pickup pulled up. Thank God. Turning on his overhead lights, he parked and jumped out. As his long-legged stride ate up the space between them, she had to glance down to keep from throwing herself into his arms.

"Brie?" His gruff voice brought tears to her eyes.

Biting her lip, she blinked. "I'm fine. I think." Avoiding his gaze, she pointed a shaky finger at the smoke-shrouded vehicle. "But I'm not sure how he is."

Reed hesitated. His dark gaze raked over her. She shivered, wondering why she always felt his look like an actual touch, a caress.

"Eldon Brashear," she said. "He started swearing when I walked over, but hasn't gotten out of his truck."

A muscle worked in Reed's jaw. He jerked his head

in a nod. Then he strode over to the pickup. She watched him go, aching from more than the crash.

"Eldon?" Yanking the rusted door open, he reached inside and disengaged the elderly man's seat belt.

Eldon's response, naturally, was to curse louder and more virulently.

Brie shook her head, sending stabs of pain through her neck. She massaged her temples.

The pickup door groaned as Reed shoved it further back on its hinges. Half lifting the older man out, Reed supported him with an arm around his waist. He walked him to the patrol car amid a string of invectives.

Once he got Eldon seated, Reed knelt in front of him and began talking in a low voice. Though Brie tried to listen, she couldn't hear. Her head throbbing now like she had a set of drums behind each eyebrow, she moved closer so she could better hear.

Her toe connected with a rock, sending it skittering across the pavement. Eldon looked up and bared his teeth at her. His glittering eyes were so rage-filled, they stopped her in her tracks.

Stunned, she stared back, then looked at Reed. What had she ever done to deserve such hatred?

The answer came quickly. Though she'd already mentioned it to Reed, it seemed too obvious. If Eldon was the stalker, the one who'd killed her mother, he wasn't taking any pains to hide it.

As if he'd read her mind, Reed met her gaze. He slowly shook his head, mouthing the words "not now." Out loud, he said, "I need to take Eldon to the hospital and have him checked."

Eldon met this statement with a second chorus of curses.

"He seems okay, but better safe than sorry." Ignoring Eldon's ranting, Reed calmly buckled the other man in and closed the door on him, cutting off his swearing midstream. Then he crossed to Brie, touching her lightly on the shoulder. For half a second, she let herself lean into his touch. "Are you sure you're all right?"

"Yes." She lied and made the mistake of nodding again, wincing as sharp stabs of pain ricocheted inside her skull. Her double vision was gone, so she figured she'd live.

Reed's hand tightened on her shoulder. "Brie?"

"Hmm?" Her mouth felt impossibly dry. "I'll be all right. I've got a picnic to go to."

"Answer my question. Are you hurt?" But instead of waiting for her answer, he propelled her over to her car, opening the passenger side door and gently pushing her into it. Then he calmly, competently ran his hands over her, searching for broken bones.

Each stroke of his fingers seared her with heat.

She bit her lip, stifling a moan. The urge to arch into his touch, to bare her skin, nearly overpowered her. It sure as hell drove her aches and pains away. She shivered, his touch making her run hot, then cold.

Impossibly, he ignored her, intent on his inspection. She obviously didn't affect him the same way. His features were set in the remote, compassionate expression of a cop. Yet as his big hands skimmed over her shoulders, down her arms, the curve of her waist, hip, his pupils dilated, his breathing quickened.

She'd bet if she leaned into him and pressed herself against him, she'd discover he wasn't as unaffected as he pretended to be.

He was only doing his job, for Pete's sake. What was wrong with her?

Finally, he finished and stepped back. "Nothing appears to be broken, but you might have whiplash. Why don't you let me take you to the hospital?"

"No. I'm fine." She licked her lips. "My entire family is expecting me."

"They'll understand if you're late. A checkup won't take too long and might be a good idea, Brie. You've just been in an accident."

"I'm fine," she said again.

He inclined his head. His dark gaze was remote. "Then go on to the picnic."

Gingerly lifting herself out of the seat, she eyed her crumpled fender dubiously. "Do you think it'll run?"

"Sure. The only damage is to your rear bumper. It's safe to drive. I'll see you there later, once I finish with this." He walked to his truck, opening the driver's side door, still watching her. Even Eldon had fallen silent, though he still glared, his expression mutinous.

"See you—oh wait." Spying her map, still open on the front seat, she gave him a rueful smile. "Before you leave, can you point me in the right direction? I know I must be near, but I can't seem to find this Heritage Park."

He pointed. "You're nearly there. You need to go that way. Two blocks, then turn right. You'll see it."

The one route she hadn't tried. Naturally.

"Thanks." Climbing into her car, she started the ignition. Reed leaned on his door, still watching her, his expression inscrutable. She raised her hand in a half-hearted wave, shifted into gear and drove off in the direction he'd indicated.

This time, finding Heritage Park was no problem. She pulled between two mammoth SUVs into a parking spot under a leafy oak tree. She got out of the car, massaging the back of her still-aching neck. Though she'd arrived later than planned, judging from the looks of things, the others were still getting things set up.

Across the green grass, groups of people clustered under the outdoor pavilion, around a huge stack of ice chests. They'd already covered one long picnic table with a series of red-and-white checked tablecloths, which rippled in the light breeze. Behind them, two huge commercial-sized grills belched smoke. She inhaled, loving the scent of charcoal and wood chips, feeling the tension, and her headache, melt away.

They couldn't have asked for better weather. Fluffy white clouds decorated the azure sky. The sun was bright and the day promised to be warm.

On the other side of the park, the men had started a tag football game. Most of them wore cut-off shorts and sneakers and some of the younger guys were shirtless, their bronze chests gleaming in the sun. Brie tried to picture Reed that way and shook her head. Could she be any more foolish?

Aunt Marilyn spotted her and waved her over. Beaming, the affection in her bright blue eyes warmed Brie's heart. She'd never had a mother, but as a child she'd often pretended her mother's ghost was with her. With her unreserved and boundless affection, Marilyn brought Brie's childish longing back.

As Brie approached, Marilyn squealed and hugged her. "Honey, I knew you'd have no problem finding this place!"

Brie smiled ruefully. "Actually, I got lost." Briefly she told her about the accident.

"Are you all right?"

"I'm fine. Just a little shaken."

"Let me see." Real concern in her voice, Marilyn stepped back and inspected her. "You look like you're all in one piece to me. No broken bones. Any aches or pains?"

In her other life, Marilyn was a nurse. Brie shook her head. The headache was almost gone. "Nope."

"Wonderful. We heal fast, you know." Still, her sharp eyes searched Brie's face. She didn't miss much, her aunt.

"We?"

"The Beswicks," and that's all her aunt would say on the subject.

Uncle Albert was with the group of men tending the massive smokers, ever-present pipe between his teeth. Spotting Brie, he waved.

"Are you ready to meet your cousins?" Marilyn sounded thrilled enough for both of them. "They've been so excited about meeting you."

Pressing her hand against her stomach briefly, Brie lifted her chin and smiled. "I'd love to."

"Ready or not, here they come. The boys are playing ball, so you can meet them later." Her aunt raised her voice and waved at a cluster of younger women heading their way. "Molly, Edie, Jennifer, Susan. Come on over here and meet Elizabeth's daughter, Brie, your long-lost cousin."

Amid a flurry of laughter and hugs, they welcomed her. Her family. They all chattered brightly. The commotion caused more people to hurry over to meet her. It seemed like they kept coming in waves. She lost track of all the relatives she met in the space of half an hour, knowing she'd never remember all their names, and hoping they'd understand.

Family. She felt a warm glow inside at the thought.

Where had these people been all her life? She couldn't help but remember all the lonely holidays she'd had, just her and her dad.

If in fact her mother had been murdered, the killer had robbed Brie of much more than a mother.

"Earth to Brie!" Her cousin Edie's lighthearted voice broke into her thoughts. "Did you bring your swimsuit?"

Brie grinned and nodded. She'd connected instantly with this cousin. Edie already felt like a good friend. "I brought it, but left it in my car. I wasn't sure if we'd be swimming."

Truth was, she'd hoped not. She felt awkward in even her one-piece tank suit, gawky and ungainly, all legs and elbows and pale skin. Edie, on the other hand, had a great tan, curvy figure, and no doubt wore a teeny bikini and looked stunning in it.

"Of course you're swimming." Edie elbowed Brie. "It'll be hot later and you'll want to cool off."

"Okay." Brie shrugged. "Sounds good to me."

Edie leaned close. In a lower voice she continued, "The pool's a great place for eye candy. The whole town is here, just about. Not just family, if you get my drift. Lots of guys our age. They'll want to jump in the water after they get done playing ball. We've got some hotties around here, believe it or not."

Hotties. Brie thought of Reed Hunter. Picturing him rising out of a pool, his muscular chest glistening with water, made her feel dizzy.

Damn it.

"Edie, Brie." Aunt Marilyn opened one of the ice chests. "Help me get this other stuff on the tables before they start slicing the meat."

They emptied ice chest after ice chest. There were bowls of potato salad, pasta salad, green salad, Jell-O salad and platters of pickles and olives, plus rolls and loaves of homemade bread. The table groaned under more food than Brie had ever seen in one place.

"Meat's ready," one of the men shouted, as if on cue.

Aunt Marilyn and her friends laughed, grabbing cookie sheets and long metal platters. "Come on, girls. Let's get the most important part of the meal on the table."

Following behind Edie, Brie grabbed a pan. When it was her turn at the smoker, she held her arms out automatically, expecting the requisite hot dogs or hamburger patties. Instead, Uncle Albert loaded her down with steaks. Thick, huge, fragrant slabs of beef. The best-looking steaks she'd ever seen in her life. Her mouth watered just looking at them.

When her pan had been filled, he winked at her and motioned the next person forward.

Chattering and laughing, the guys abandoned their ball game and clustered near the food. Brie found herself searching their faces, looking for one in particular.

"Look who just got here." Several of the teenage girls giggled, hands over their mouths. "He's so cuuute."

She heard a car door slam and turned to see Reed emerging from his pickup.

"Ah, he's fine to look at, but watch out for that one." Edie stared at Reed as he sauntered over to them. Unlike Brie, her pretty face bore an expression of distaste.

"Why?" Brie wanted to know about Reed. "He seems like a nice guy to me."

"Oh, he's nice." Pursing her lips, Edie shook her head. "Nice to look at, nice to talk to. But that's it. Don't get involved with him. That's only asking for trouble. Everyone in town knows that. Mothers warn their daughters away from Hunter men."

"What?" Puzzled, Brie looked from Reed to her cousin, and back again. "Explain. Please."

Edie looked her in the face, her bright gaze missing nothing. "Don't tell me you—"

"No! Nothing like that. I…" Swallowing, Brie shook her head. "I'm attracted to him, that's all. I'd like to know if there's a good reason I shouldn't be."

"A good reason!" Her cousin all but crowed. "Honey, if you value your life, you'll stay away from him. He's cursed. His family has been for generations. Everyone knows about the Hunter curse. Any woman who gets involved with Reed Hunter will wind up dead. His wife found that out too late."

Was she kidding? But her expression looked serious. Brie grabbed Edie's arm, as the rest of her words registered. "His *wife*? What on earth are you talking about?"

Edie cut her eyes. "Shh."

A shadow fell over them. Brie looked up to meet Reed's smoky gaze. Her heart somersaulted in her chest.

"Brie." Unsmiling, he continued to study her. "I need to talk to you for a minute."

Edie looked from one to the other, pursing her lips. Her lovely eyes were hard. "Don't mind me, I'm leaving." She tugged at Brie's short hair. "Brie, remember what I said. Please. We'll talk more later." Cutting another sharp look at Reed, she strolled off.

Reed watched her go, a resigned look on his rugged face. "I can imagine what she's been saying."

"She was just telling me about your curse." Though

Brie meant the comment lightly, there was nothing light about the shadow that crossed his eyes.

"I see." He didn't elaborate, or ask Brie to either. "I just left Eldon Brashear at the hospital. He wants to press charges. He says he thinks you're stalking him."

Had the entire world gone crazy? "Me? Reed, he rear-ended me. I was stopped at the stop sign, minding my own business. If anyone's stalking anyone, he's the one who was following me."

The scent of meat smoking drifted over to tantalize her nose, reminding her they were about to eat.

"I tried to tell him he was acting foolishly, but he's insisting."

"What will happen?"

"Probably nothing. No one, once they read my accident report, will take him seriously. But he's acting worse than normal, even for him. I thought I'd better warn you."

"Warning duly noted." No way was she letting that crazy man ruin her day. If he was the letter writer, he couldn't bother her now, since he wasn't here.

She looked up to find Reed staring down at her, his expression unreadable. "What's wrong?"

"Nothing." Swallowing, he glanced away from her, to where her cousins watched them intently. "I think I'd better go."

"Go where? You're just in time for the food." She touched his arm, reveling in the jolt the contact brought. Maybe it was delayed reaction from the accident, but she felt bold, all of a sudden. And she was happier to see him than she had a right to be.

"I think they," he indicated Edie and the other cousins with a jerk of his head, "would be happier if I leave."

"No, they wouldn't. Stay." She touched him again, smiling as he jumped. "Please. At least you should eat."

"I think I will." Brushing past her, he grabbed a paper plate and got in line. Unable to keep her expression serious, Brie did the same.

Later, after they'd devoured the repast, they waited in line again to get to the big trash barrels. Right behind Reed, Brie dumped her plate and turned in time to see a small group of men disappearing into the woods.

Edie noticed her watching. "They're going for a run," she said with a smile. "Sometimes the guys like to do that, especially after they've had so much red meat. It makes for Pack bonding."

"Pack bonding?" Brie stumbled over the unfamiliar words. "Is this a New York thing? What's it mean?"

Edie opened her mouth to answer.

"Edie," Reed's sharp voice cut her off. "Enough."

With a shrug, Edie complied. Shooting Reed a glare, she marched off to join her friends. Reed watched her go, as expressionless as he'd been before.

"What was that all about?" Brie asked. He ignored her, staring at the spot where the men had vanished into the trees. Was he wishing he could join them?

"Reed? Tell me about this curse."

He snapped his head around, expression grim. "I'd rather not."

"In a town this small, I'm sure to find out sooner or later. I'd rather hear it from you." She smiled, aching to touch him again but sure she'd better not. "It's a joke, right? Some kind of gag?"

"You sound as though you don't believe in curses." His eyes went flat and cold.

"Do you?"

"I have to."

His reaction intrigued her. "Really? Now you've got to explain. Why do you have to?"

He laughed: a short bark of sound that held no humor. "In all fairness, I suppose most rational people don't believe there could be such a thing as a curse."

"But you do?"

"Hell hounds, Brie, I wish I didn't." He started walking, away from her cousin's censuring gaze.

Brie hurried to keep up with him. "Hell hounds?"

He looked away, his jaw tight. "It's an expression."

They'd reached the other side of the baseball diamond. More forest lay beyond, wild and untamed. Reed stopped, leaning against a tree, his back to her. For a second, Brie wondered about the men she'd seen disappear into the forest. Pack bonding? She filed that question away for another time. Right now, she wanted to know about the curse.

"Tell me about this curse, and why you believe it. Please."

He didn't turn to look at her. "I used to think it was a bunch of crap, even when I was small and the other kids teased me. When the girls weren't allowed to be my friend, and I wasn't even allowed to date or take a girl to prom."

He sounded so bleak, she longed to go to him, wrap her arms around his waist and hold him. Of course she didn't. She had to keep reminding herself she barely knew the man.

He fell silent for so long she wondered if he was going to continue. When he looked at her, she saw hopelessness in his eyes. Finally, he spoke. "I don't know where to start."

"Start at the beginning."

"The Hunter family was cursed so long ago no one remembers who cursed us. As for the particulars, it's simple. Any woman who has a close relationship with a Hunter male will die a horrible death. Some have characterized that as friendship, others, sex. Either way, women around here avoid me. I'm surprised they even let me go off to college. My uncle Malcolm is the only family I have left. He's a priest, so when he insisted, I got to go. But even he talked to me before I left. Warned me of the consequences, were I to allow a woman to get close."

At the raw pain in his voice, Brie shivered. He truly believed what he was saying. "Reed—"

"Generations of my family have suffered because of this damn curse. We are shunned, and if we wish to marry, we do so knowing we risk the poor woman's life." His harsh voice broke.

Finally, tentatively, she asked. "And you believe this, too?"

"I didn't, not at first." Each word seemed to be wrung from him with pincers. "Even though my own mother died in a car accident, even though my brother Danny and his wife both perished in a fire at their home. Even though I grieved for them, I still didn't believe. A curse? No way. Extremely bad luck, maybe. A horrible chain of events, one family's suffering. I hurt, yes, but in my heart of hearts I didn't believe in the curse."

Brie could only stare. She wasn't sure she wanted to know more. "Then what?"

"Then I met Teresa. My wife."

Wife. Odd how such a simple word could twist her stomach so. "I didn't know you were married."

"Was." He gave her the look a convicted man must wear when he's strapped into the electric chair. "Teresa's dead. She died nearly three years ago."

Oh God, the curse.

"Yes, the curse." Head bowed as though he still grieved, he rubbed the back of his neck.

She must have spoken out loud again.

"The curse has ruined the lives of everyone in my family. Except for my uncle Malcolm. He's the only one who has managed to remain untouched by the curse. He's the only one who had sense enough not to marry."

Reed scanned the crowd. He pointed to a tall man in a black jacket and a cleric's collar, surrounded by several other, older men. "There he is. I'll take you to meet him later, when he's not so busy."

She nodded. "One thing you haven't told me. How can this curse be broken?"

He turned to face her, the starkness of his expression breaking Brie's heart. "You've seen the church?"

She nodded.

"There's a bell in the tower. The curse will be broken when the bell cracks while ringing to announce a Hunter male's marriage, once he has been wed. So no one knows if the curse has been lifted until after they've wed."

"The bell in the...?" Brie wrapped her arms around her middle to keep from touching him. "I don't understand the connection."

"No one remembers what it is. But there is one, even if the reason is another thing that got lost over time."

A soccer ball whacked her in the knee. Startled, Brie jumped, then bent over and retrieved the ball. A small, towheaded boy ran over and held his arms out for the ball.

"What do you say?" she teased, holding the prize out of his reach.

The little boy grinned at her. And growled.

Shocked, Brie dropped the ball. "What the…"

"Riley, get over here." His frazzled mother, a petite blond woman who was visibly pregnant, called him back. Brie thought she might be one of her cousins, but couldn't remember, there'd been so many. "Tell Brie you're sorry."

Kicking his shoes into the dirt, he scowled up at her. "Sorry, Brie." He sounded anything but.

"It's okay. Go on back to your mother now." Brie reached out to give Riley a gentle push in the right direction. Instead of going, he snapped at her, just like a wild animal—like a dog.

"Riley." Hurrying over, his mother snatched him away and marched him off, all the while calling out apologies.

Reed shook his head and muttered something that sounded like *young whelp*.

Two other small children, who'd been watching from a distance, giggled and shyly approached Brie.

"Riley says you haven't changed yet." The smallest one, a dark haired little girl with skin the color of caramel skipped over. "Is that true?"

"Changed?" Brie shook her head, bending down so she could meet the child's gaze. "I don't understand. What do you mean?"

Instead of answering, the little girl squealed, "It's true, it's true. I told you so." Racing off, the two kids shouted at each other all the way back to their parents.

Changed. Brie thought back to the other time she'd been asked that question. By Reed, when she'd first arrived in town. She'd thought then he'd meant was she different from the infant she'd been when she'd left town. Now she wondered if he'd meant changed in another sense, something completely different and more sinister.

She looked at him, watching with his impassive, cop face. "I think you owe me another explanation. What is this change everyone keeps talking about? What does it mean?"

He raised a brow. "Let me tell you something, Brie Danzinger. If you have trouble believing in my family's curse, there's no way you'd believe the truth about changing. No way at all."

Chapter 6

"How old is Reed Hunter?" Brie asked her aunt later. "He said he knew my mother, but he doesn't seem so old."

Aunt Marilyn laughed. "Reed was about eight when your mother died."

"He seems so... lonely."

The older woman's sharp gaze missed nothing. "That comes with being a Hunter. No one wants their sister or daughter to mingle with him. He's worked hard to make himself less of an outcast. Came back here after graduating from college with a wife. He started out as a police officer, and worked his way up to chief."

"People seem to like him."

"They do. He's a good guy. There was concern when his wife died, a lot of anger too. His uncle Malcolm diffused the situation for him. He made Reed swear a public oath, to leave the females alone."

Shocked, Brie pressed a hand to her stomach. "While he was still grieving his own wife's death?"

"Yes." The stubborn set of Marilyn's chin told Brie her aunt agreed with this. "It's important. As long as he stays away from women, he'll be accepted." With a concerned expression, she hugged Brie close. "Brie, for Cerberus's sake, you're not interested in him, are you?"

"Cerberus's sake? I've heard some weird expressions here, but that one takes the cake. What's it mean?"

"Greek mythology. The three-headed dog guarding the gates to Hades." Still frowning, Marilyn would not be distracted. "Brie, answer the question. You're not interested in Reed Hunter, are you?"

"No," Brie answered, too quickly. "Of course not. But it sounds like you believe in this curse, too. That's crazy."

Marilyn's expression changed. "Honey, the Hunter family's curse is real. Women who love a Hunter die. Generation after generation of Hunter women have died horrific deaths."

"I don't understand. Has no one ever tried to find out why, or to try and break this supposed curse?"

"I've been researching it over the years," Marilyn said slowly. "There's been a rumor that one of our ancestors was the one who cursed them, though I haven't been able to prove or disprove that, or to find out why. I'm the keeper of our Beswick family history."

"A Beswick? Interesting. That brings to mind another question." Brie was all questions today. "Why is it tradition to keep the Beswick name, even when you marry?"

"Honey, it just is. That's the way we Beswicks do things. It's been that way since our ancestors landed on these shores. Our husbands accept this. Except," the older woman looked Brie up and down, "your father. He didn't let you keep your true name."

"We hyphenated the name, until I got old enough to ask if I could just be a Danzinger, like him. That was my choice, not his." She couldn't tell her aunt the rest of it—that her father had deemed it safer if she hid the Beswick part of her name.

"About the curse." Doggedly, Marilyn continued on track. "Reed lost his wife to that curse."

"He mentioned that."

Her aunt pursed her lips. "I'm shocked. He never talks about that. Not since Teresa died." Marilyn gazed at the baseball diamond, where the younger men were playing a vigorous game against the older ones. Most of the women watched, cheering them on. Aunt Marilyn had stayed behind to keep an eye on the multiple ice-cream makers that were churning. Brie had waited with her, glad of the opportunity to talk in private.

"There are a lot of things in this world that might seem beyond belief, but they're true." Aunt Marilyn winked at her as she spoke. "So stay away from Reed Hunter."

"I'll keep that in mind." Brie nodded. "I do have one more question."

"Another one?" Marilyn grimaced. "Don't you ever get tired?"

"Last one of the day, I promise." Keeping her voice casual, Brie watched closely for her aunt's reaction. "When people ask me if I've changed, what exactly do they mean?"

Instantly, Marilyn went still, her freckled complexion going dusty red as she peered into Brie's face. "Who's been asking you that?"

Brie shrugged, brushing away a dragonfly. "Kids. Other people, here and there. Can you tell me what it means?"

"Er, no. I can't."

"But you do know?"

"Yes."

Brie waited. Aunt Marilyn stared back, impassive.

Finally, Brie sighed. "Why won't anyone tell me? I want to find out. It's driving me crazy."

"When you're ready, you'll know."

"Right. Curses and secrets. I feel like I'm back in Boulder, getting handed pamphlets and philosophy on Pearl Street."

The reference to the eclectic street in Boulder was lost on the older woman. She'd never been out of Leaning Tree.

A roar came from the group at the baseball diamond. Apparently, the group that had disappeared into the woods had returned. Brie looked up to see Reed, laughing, trot past second base. She felt a pang of longing, so sharp she nearly gasped out loud. What was it about this man? Why did he affect her so strongly?

"Brie? Are you all right?"

She looked back to see her aunt studying her.

"I'm tired. If it's okay with you, I think I'll go now." Brie kissed Marilyn's plump cheek.

"Oh no, you don't." The flush had faded from Marilyn's face. Whatever secrets she kept hidden weren't visible in her pleasant smile. "You can't go. You're the guest of honor and—more important—you haven't tasted my homemade peach ice cream yet. There's nothing like it, I promise you."

Brie hesitated, her glance going to Reed. Merely

looking at him filled her with an indefinable ache so strong it made her want to weep.

Damn it.

"Brie?" Fiddling with one of the ice-cream makers, Aunt Marilyn straightened. "You can't go yet. There will be swimming later."

As much as Brie would've liked to deny it, the thought of seeing Reed in a swimsuit decided her. "You've convinced me," she said, smiling. "I'll stay a little longer."

The next day Brie woke up content. The sound of her aunt and uncle talking over coffee made her feel at home. She'd never felt so accepted, so much a part of things. Her family, heck, the entire town, was special. Every single person she'd met seemed to welcome her.

Except Eldon Brashear. Though normally, she'd consider him a prime suspect as her mother's stalker, she doubted the man could write her a complimentary letter to save his life. So the letter writer had to be someone else.

Climbing out of bed, she pulled on a pair of terry cloth shorts and a T-shirt, then went to the kitchen to join her aunt and uncle for coffee.

"Good morning, sleepyhead." Marilyn kissed her on the cheek. "You're too late for services, so I'm thinking you weren't planning on going to church."

Pouring herself a mug of coffee, Brie shook her head. "No, I wasn't. I met Father Malcolm yesterday and he invited me to see the church. I'd planned on touring it today, but forgot today was Sunday."

"The services don't last all day," Albert put in. "And showing newcomers around is one of Father Malcolm's greatest pleasures."

"Yes, he so enjoys the chance to show off our beautiful church." Marilyn slid a plate of Danishes across the counter. "Why don't you go?" Her mouth twisted. "You might as well see the place where your mother should have been buried."

"Marilyn." Albert's warning was sharp. "That's enough. Don't prejudice the girl. None of this is Malcolm's fault."

"No, it isn't." Sitting down heavily, Marilyn sighed. "Father Malcolm is a good man. He has no choice but to follow the dictates of the church."

Brie nodded. "I might just do that. I would really like to see the place." She'd been impressed by Father Malcolm. A distinguished older man, he wore his hair long for a priest, and the touches of gray at his temples added to his roguish appeal. He was soft-spoken, like most priests, and charming. She looked forward to spending some time with him. Maybe he would answer some of her questions.

"Why don't you do that, dear." Marilyn sipped from her cup. "But eat something first."

An hour later, showered and fed, Brie got into her car. The drive downtown took less than five minutes. Parking by the root beer stand, she went straight around the church building, heading toward the cemetery, wanting to check that out first. With the overcast skies and the breeze carrying a trace of northern sharpness, she imagined she might be in Ireland or some other country where history seeps up through the ground. The old churchyard carried that kind of feeling, as if secrets had been deposited there over the ages.

Made of slate stone, the small, rectangular building gave off an air of age and reassuring sturdiness. A small plaque on one corner proclaimed the building had been built by Dutch settlers in the late 1600s. The steeple and belfry had been added a bit later—built specifically to house the bell itself.

The sheer age of the structures astounded her. In Colorado, most of the old buildings in Boulder dated from the 1800s. She knew of an old mission church from much earlier, but that was farther south, below Colorado Springs. Nothing like this. Nothing that felt so old.

Trailing one hand over the mottled rock, she smiled at its smoothness. Worn by age, it felt like river stone, polished by water and wind rather than the hand of man.

Finally she reached the back side of the building and the cemetery. Opening the creaky metal gate, she went inside, wandering between and around the graves while the wind tossed the leaves on the ancient trees. Though well-tended, some of the tombstones were so old that the inscriptions had been rendered indecipherable, wiped clean by time.

On and among the stone markers, she noted a plethora of wolf statues, which seemed odd. She'd thought the one carved into her mother's headstone had been beautiful, but it had been the only wolf she'd noticed in that particular cemetery. Here, mingled with the occasional stone angel or cross, there were hundreds of them. Wolves howling, sitting, crouching and hunting. These beasts decorated most of the tombstones, the vaults and the benches. A giant wolf statue watched over the cemetery rather than the usual angel. Why wolves? She'd ask the priest. Surely there was a story behind them.

Despite the eerie atmosphere and her sad certainty that her mother belonged here with the rest of her family, as Brie walked among the old burial grounds, a sense of peace stole over her. She strolled among the graves, reading what stones she could, and marveling at the generations of townspeople buried here. Buried where they'd spent their entire lives. Living with such permanence amazed her and pleased her.

"Good morning." The soft-spoken, sonorous voice came from behind her, making her jump.

Father Malcolm. She hadn't heard a thing. Shaking her head, she peered up at him. "Hi! You know, people around here are really good at sneaking up on a person."

"I apologize." His smile was soft. "Perhaps you were so engrossed in your study of the graves, you didn't hear me coming."

She smiled back. "That must have been it. What a beautiful cemetery you have here."

"Thank you." His smile broadened. Today he wore a flowing black cassock and looked very priestly. "Would you like to come inside? I have fresh, hot coffee."

"I'd like that." She followed him through the side door. Once inside, she stopped, awestruck. She drank in the beauty of the sunlight pouring through the stained glass windows, the sheen and gloss of the polished oak pews, the comforting creak of the warm wood floor. In such a place one truly felt holy, almost worthy of communing with a higher power.

"Beautiful, isn't it?" Though he spoke quietly, Father Malcolm's voice reverberated around the small church. His rich tones suited his chosen occupation.

"Amazingly so."

She followed him to the rectory, noting the stairs that led up to the belfry were roped off. They passed through the classrooms, down a short hall and turned right. He closed the sliding, wooden door that separated his living area from the rest of the church.

Still, even in the fairly modern surroundings, she could feel the press of age emanating from the stone walls.

"Living here must feel like an ongoing history lesson."

Her statement didn't even make him blink. "It is." Pouring them both mugs of coffee, he took a sip with a sigh of obvious pleasure. "Starbucks," he said. "One of my parishioners just got back from Seattle."

Accepting the hot mug, Brie added two lumps of sugar and a teaspoon of powdered creamer.

"Have a seat." He indicated a couple of old, wooden, folding chairs in front of a beat-up, metal desk. They appeared quite sturdy.

Brie took one, he took the other. They creaked as they sat.

Once again, Brie felt a sense of being at home. "I hope you don't mind my showing up unannounced."

"Not at all. After all, young lady, I invited you yesterday. I enjoy showing newcomers around. Most of us here in town have grown up with this church, so we're too accustomed to her. This often makes us blind to her beauty."

"I don't see how," Brie said honestly. "It's lovely."

"You came here today to tour the church?"

Sipping slowly, Brie fiddled with her bracelet. "Yes. And I wanted to see the place where my mother should have been buried."

Father Malcolm sighed. "I apologize, but you know the Church's stance on suicide. Your mother could not be allowed to rest in hallowed ground."

"She didn't kill herself."

Pity showed in his eyes. "I'm sorry, Brie."

"Did you know my mother?"

He gave her a startled look. "Of course I did. I went to school with her." Leaning forward, he placed his hand on top of hers. "I liked your mother, Brie. Everyone in town did."

Suddenly, perilously close to tears, Brie nodded.

"Well." He set his cup down with a thunk. "Would you like a tour of the church?"

"Sure." A quick look around, then she'd make a hasty exit. Father Malcolm was a nice enough man. He had no choice but to go by the dictates of his church. Her mother's death had been ruled a suicide. Until she found proof otherwise, that was the way it had to be. For now, she'd have to agree to disagree with him on the subject of her mother's burial.

He stood. "I could even show you the bell, if you'd like. It's quite old and very majestic."

"The bell? The one that won't break?" The second she'd spoken, she wanted to call back the words.

"That very one." He pinched his nose with his left hand. "You are aware I'm a Hunter as well?"

"Yes." She winced. "I'm sorry. I keep forgetting how seriously everyone takes that curse."

"Sometimes they don't take it seriously enough." He looked old suddenly. Old and tired. "What do you know about the curse? What did my nephew tell you?"

"I know the curse has taken its toll on the women who marry into your family." Humoring him, she smiled. "But you don't have to worry about that, do you?"

"No. Of course not." Reaching for his cup, he drank deeply, downing the coffee the way another man might gulp whiskey. "That's one of the reasons I joined the priesthood. That, and an abiding spiritual call, naturally."

She glanced around the spartan room. A large, wooden cross on one wall was the only decoration. "How do you reconcile the two? The church and this curse?"

He shook his head, smiling faintly. "The Church has her own share of mysteries. My family's curse is nothing compared to some of them."

Brie decided to let it go. Obviously she was the only skeptic in town. "About that tour?"

He set his coffee cup down. "Certainly. Come with me. Showing you around will only take a few minutes."

The tour of the sanctuary was short, as promised. Brie was shocked as she realized there were wolf images in the stained glass and wooden wolf heads had been carved in the end of every pew.

"Father Malcolm?" She waited until they'd reached the back of the building, where hundreds of candles burned. They'd been placed on graduating risers.

He turned, his long cassock swirling around him, his expression serene. "Yes?" He raised one brow in question.

Brie felt she was looking at Reed in thirty years. "Why wolves?" She indicated the pews, the windows. "I noticed them outside too, in the cemetery."

"Wolves are our token animal." He smiled. "We are quite fond of them around here."

"I've noticed. But they don't seem very churchlike, do they?" she persisted. "One normally thinks of angels and cherubs, heavenly beings."

"We prefer wolves." With a shrug, he indicated the subject was closed. He led the way to the front door. "Well, that's my little tour."

"What about the bell?" No way was she leaving without seeing that.

"I almost forgot." His smile was gentle. "This way, please."

She followed as he pushed aside the heavy, velvet rope and unlocked a thick, wooden door with an old-fashioned key. Silently, they climbed the narrow, twisting staircase. The wood creaked with each step. When they finally reached the top, the priest was barely winded. Brie, on the other hand, gasped like a fish out of water.

Another wooden door, exactly like the first, blocked the way. Using another key from a brass ring, Father Malcolm unlocked it. "Here we are." His tone was reverent, proud.

Despite the stories, she was unprepared for the actual sight of the bell. Even in the shadowy belfry, the massive brass bell glowed dully.

Her first impression was that of overwhelming age. Though she knew it was impossible, the bell seemed far older than the building itself, older than the ships which had delivered the first settlers to the New York shores, older even than the ones who'd been displaced by them. Celtic perhaps. Maybe even Roman.

Taken aback at her wild thoughts, Brie inhaled deeply. Such a thing wasn't even remotely possible. What did she know, anyway? She was no judge of antiquities.

But her gut instincts had never led her astray before.

She blinked. None of this mattered. She felt a pull, strong, compelling. The bell, dark and mysterious, called to her. Awestruck, she moved closer, ignoring the priest's words of caution. Close enough to touch the brass, to reach out her hand—noting with surprise how she trembled—and lay her fingers flush against the cool metal.

Old—ancient. Such a thing could easily carry a curse. But this… Instead of a sense of evil, the softest sensation of comfort stole over her. Of serenity. A quiet sense of joy.

Gradually, she became aware Father Malcolm was calling her name.

"Brie?" The enveloping calm vanished when his hand came down on her shoulder. She whipped her head up. A flash of blinding rage made her want to strike his hand from her, to wipe away his touch. She blinked, bit down on the side of her cheek so hard it hurt, and inhaled a shaky breath. What the heck? Where had that come from?

He'd seen, too. The priest had taken a step away from her, removing his hand of his own accord. He watched her now with something akin to fear.

"I'm sorry." Moving blindly, Brie made it to the stairwell. "I didn't…"

Her footsteps clattered as she rushed down, careless of potential danger, heedless of everything except the frantic touch of panic that always heralded an attack.

When she reached the bottom, she stopped, willing herself calm, trying to force away the churning emotions clutching at her insides.

Father Malcolm didn't immediately follow. After a few minutes, she heard the clank and clatter of his keys as he locked the first door at the top of the stairs.

Chest heaving, she waited for him, just inside the rectory. Breathing in, breathing out, trying to make sense of what had happened up in the belfry.

After locking the bottom door and tucking the keys in a pocket in his voluminous robe, he turned and faced her.

"What happened to you? Are you all right?"

She shook her head, ashamed and bemused and now fighting off the first waves of panic. "I can't… I don't know what…"

"Easy, child."

But he couldn't calm her. The panic she'd been holding at bay suddenly broke loose, suffocating her. A full-blown panic attack—here and now.

"I've got to go." Not even pretending to be civil, she rushed out into the gray, gloomy day, and the haven her car had suddenly become.

Chapter 7

As Brie climbed inside her Mazda, fat drops of rain began to pummel the windshield. She barely noticed.

She fought herself, fought the urge to run blindly, knowing she couldn't flee when the panic came from within. Shaking, gasping for air, she clenched her jaw, hard.

Out of reflex, she locked the door, but though she clutched the key in her shaking hand, she didn't put it in the ignition. There was no point. She couldn't drive in the throes of an attack—she'd nearly wrecked her car trying when she was seventeen. Instead, she ground her teeth and slammed her head back against the headrest.

Closing her eyes, taking deep, shuddering breaths, she began chanting, two words over and over again. Though the words themselves didn't matter as it was the endless repetition she found calming, she spoke words that mattered to her. A lot.

"No fear," she said. "No fear, no fear, no fear, no fear." Over and over, blotting out everything but the cadence of her voice repeating the words.

When finally, minutes or hours later, she opened her eyes, she'd stopped trembling. She could breathe normally again and her heartbeat had resumed its steady and sure rhythm. Now, she could drive. Fumbling with the key, she got it into the ignition and started the car.

Surprised to find tears on her cheeks, she wiped her face and sniffed.

Instead of heading back to her aunt's house, she took the two-lane road south out of town, wanting to drive until she became calmer.

The skies opened up and it began to pour. She flipped her wipers on high. With a slow headache building behind her temples, she kept both hands on the wheel as she concentrated on the winding road. Her thoughts kept returning to the church and what had happened with the bell. Even thinking about it brought a fine-edged sense of longing. She saw again in her mind's eye the brass appearing to glow softly. The bell. The beautiful, cursed, bell.

Her agitation returned, palpable, but not yet panic. When she got back to Aunt Marilyn's, she needed to walk in the woods. Even in the rain, the woods, dark and peaceful, beckoned with a promise of peace. Aunt Marilyn's acre of land was supposed to be safe. She'd promised she wouldn't roam around anywhere else alone.

After hearing about the incident with Eldon Brashear, her aunt had warned her against traipsing around other people's land without permission.

Slowing to negotiate a sharp curve, Brie spotted a blur of movement ahead, on the grassy shoulder. Peering through the blinding rain, she saw a small animal. Was it a dog? She slowed even more.

As she drew closer, she realized someone had dumped a puppy off alongside the road. The cardboard box they'd used had tipped over and torn. The puppy, a large black-and-tan mongrel, darted across the road in front of her.

She cursed and swerved. Heart pounding, she pulled over onto the shoulder. The rain drummed on her roof. Steeling herself, she jumped out of the car. Still reeling from her encounter with the bell, her legs threatened to buckle under her.

Instantly soaked, she lost sight of the puppy—it must have run into the underbrush. She'd have to go in after it—there was no question of leaving the young dog— it would starve out here so far from town, assuming something bigger didn't get it first.

Despite her aunt's warnings about predatory wildlife and proprietary humans, she went crashing into the forest after the pup.

As soon as she dove into the forest, the wide-limbed trees provided shelter from the downpour. Continuing on, she heard the dog ahead of her, crashing through the accumulation of last fall's leaves.

As she crept through the soggy underbrush, carefully parting rain-soaked branches, she thought she could see the puppy ahead. If this lost dog was like most small animals, soon it would tire of exploring and settle down to rest. Then she could swoop in and rescue it.

There it was. Sitting under a large brush, taking shelter from the rain.

Closer and closer she moved on her unsuspecting target. Ten feet. Five. Then she stepped on a rock and stumbled. The puppy jumped and sprinted up a small incline.

Brie raced after it, slipping and sliding on the saturated earth. When she scrabbled up the crest of the hill on her knees, she saw not one, but three small animals. Her heart sank. They weren't dogs. Not even close.

They were wolf cubs. And they were guarded by the biggest adult she-wolf she'd ever seen in her life.

Crap.

The mother wolf rose to her feet and snarled.

Brie began to slowly, slowly back away.

Bam. A shot rang out. Bam. Another.

Crouching low, ears flat against her skull, the she-wolf shot Brie a glance, then ran, herding her babies with nips of her sharp teeth.

She heard the crack of another shot. Was that only her imagination, or had a bullet just whizzed past her? Was the shooter aiming for the wolves, or for her?

Trespassers are shot around here.

They might be shooting at the wolves. Or not. Taking no chances, Brie dropped to the ground and began to backtrack the way she'd come on her knees.

A fourth shot. How many bullets did a gun have? She tried to remember. Six? Or did they make them with more, these days? Not being a gun aficionado, she wasn't sure. Best bet—remain on her hands and knees and crawl.

Once she reached the gully that marked the embankment at the road, Brie jumped up and ran like hell. Got her car started and in gear without hearing another shot.

As she stomped the accelerator to the floor, her rear window shattered. She swore.

Speeding away, she pushed the Mazda to its limits.

Driving well over the speed limit, she prayed some cop would radar her and pull her over. Of course, none did. So she did the next best thing. If they wouldn't come to her, she'd go to them. Though it was a miracle she could keep the car on the road with the way her hands were shaking, she drove straight to the police department.

Reed looked up when she ran in. From his startled expression, she knew she must have looked a sight—disheveled and sopping wet, leaf-covered, wild-eyed and trembling.

"Brie!" He grabbed her. "What happened? Are you okay?"

Keeping her voice tight and controlled, she told him an abbreviated version of what had happened. He listened, arms crossed. Then she led him outside in the rain to see her busted rear window.

Jaw tight, he completed a circle around the car. When he finally looked at her, his expression was grim. "Brie, I know your aunt Marilyn warned you about hunters. Why'd you go into someone else's woods?" Concern shone from his dark eyes.

"It was the puppy. I saw what I thought was an abandoned puppy by the side of the road. I couldn't leave it there to starve or get eaten by some bigger animal."

"You went after a puppy?"

"I thought it was a puppy." She swallowed, knowing he'd scoff when he heard the truth. "Turned out it was a wolf cub."

Reed went absolutely still. Like a pissed-off statue. "You saw a *wolf cub*?"

"I know it sounds weird, but I did. Actually, I stum-

bled across an entire litter of them, mama wolf and all."
Then, because he didn't immediately reply, she continued. "At least it wasn't the stalker." There. At least she'd
found something positive in the whole thing.

"How do you know?" Reed's voice vibrated with
anger.

"I've done a little research. Unless this guy is a true
psychopath, stalkers tend to follow a pattern. They write
a lot of letters, mostly complimentary, before something sets them off. I've only gotten one letter and, as
far as I know, done nothing to set the guy off."

"You're looking into your mother's death. That's reason enough, don't you think?"

"No one knows about that besides you. No, whoever
shot at me might have been shooting at the wolves,
though I doubt it. My car didn't get hit by accident. I
was nowhere near them." She heaved a sigh. "My insurance company is going to love this. I've still got to get
my side window repaired from the other day."

"Shooting at the wolves. That's impossible."

"Maybe around here." She regarded him curiously.
"Since everyone seems to love them. By the way, what's
up with that? I asked your Uncle Malcolm, but he didn't
give me a good answer."

Neither, it appeared, would Reed. He changed the
subject. "Where was this?"

She told him the approximate location. "And if you
tell me Eldon Brashear owns land out that way, I'm
telling you that you need to arrest him."

He gave her a grim smile. "No, not Eldon. That
acreage out there belongs to Scott Wells. He's the guy
your mother broke up with to marry your father."

"What?" Brie stared. "My mother had a serious boyfriend? Why didn't you mention that earlier? I'd have considered him a suspect. For all you know, he could be the stalker."

"I doubt that. Scott is a steady guy. Farms the land, keeps to himself."

"Still," she insisted, "we need to go talk to him."

"Oh, we will. But not about writing letters. I need to find out if he's been using wolves for target practice. That's against the law here. So help me, if I find out he owns a twelve-gauge…"

She waited for him to complete the sentence. Instead, he spun on his heel and headed back inside the police station. One of his officers, Greg Saucier, stepped aside for them to pass. Brie smiled at him. "Thanks."

"Come on," Reed growled, leading the way to his office.

She followed. "Where's your receptionist?"

"Tammy had a doctor's appointment." He slammed the door closed.

Looking up at him, Brie opened her mouth to ask him why so many people around here seemed to shoot first and ask questions later.

But he stopped her cold. He kissed her instead.

Reed hadn't meant to kiss her, but when she faced him with her chest heaving, full lips parted, he couldn't help himself. After seeing her rush in, looking like she'd narrowly escaped being mauled to death, his adrenaline was high—roaring through his blood and bringing his need to change closer to the surface than he'd ever allowed it to be around humans.

She might have been killed.

And she didn't even seem to realize this. Or care.

When he finally lifted his mouth from hers, one of his hands had become entangled in her shirt. She'd brought her arms up around his neck, and their bodies were molded together, breast to breast, hip to hip.

It felt good. Really good, in fact. Right.

She gazed up at him, those incredible azure eyes glazed with desire, and Reed realized if he didn't move, he'd risk placing her life in even greater jeopardy.

The curse.

He jumped back as though she'd bit him.

"I'm sorry—I apologize." As he ran his hand through his hair, fury ripped through him, fueling the adrenaline. His control was precarious and shaky. Lust and confusion warred with his anger. If he didn't get outside and into the woods, he might change right there in front of her.

Still she stared, saying nothing. Slowly, she brought one hand up to her mouth and touched her swollen lips. She whimpered.

This was nearly his undoing. He swallowed hard to keep from groaning out loud.

Damn it. Damn her. Damn the curse.

"Leave," he snarled.

Her eyes went wide with shock.

Then, because he couldn't argue, couldn't wait for her to decide whether to do as he asked, he pushed past her. He hit the front door running, and lengthened his stride as he neared the woods.

As soon as the underbrush closed around him, he tore off his clothes, tossed them on a rock and let the urge take over. His blood boiled as his body stretched, bones lengthening, and changing.

Then he was wolf. Animal. His strength a heady thing, he ran full out, crashing through the rain-soaked underbrush, not caring how much noise he made. He ran as though he could escape her, ran as though thoughts of her didn't pursue him even now, even here, as his other self.

Brie, Brie, Brie.

He wanted her, needed her, felt a connection to her which he hadn't felt in...ever. He couldn't feel this way, yet he did. Couldn't, wouldn't, shouldn't, not with the curse that hung over him and any woman he claimed as his own.

Later, much later, energy and lust purged from him in a bloody feeding frenzy, he returned to the glade where he'd dropped his uniform. Night had fallen, the rain stopped, the moon was hidden behind water-heavy clouds. In full darkness he changed back to human, lying exhausted on the cool, wet ground, panting. Then he climbed to his feet, dressed, and returned to the police station. Though a light still burned, the parking lot was empty—Brie was long gone.

No doubt wondering where he'd gotten off to, Tammy must have returned and locked the place up. Reed checked the locks and made sure everything was secure before he went home to his empty house. Like always. Alone. It was better that way.

Kissing her had made Reed run away in horror. Unable to believe it, Brie had stared after him, going to the doorway and watching as he'd taken off for destinations unknown. She'd caused various reactions in men, but never such an extremely adverse one.

Worse, despite her effect on him, kissing him had curled her toes. Aching, she'd wanted more, much more. Curse and bell be damned.

Obviously, she hadn't had quite the same effect on him. She told herself it was his loss, not hers, but knew she was lying. She'd never been in the habit of lying to herself. She wouldn't start now.

He had to return soon. They needed to talk about this. She'd only just met him, but felt as if she'd known him forever. Plus, she had a ton of questions about this Scott Wells person. Had he been investigated when her mother had died?

Restless, she paced while she waited over an hour for him to come back, but the only one who showed up was Tammy, who appeared decidedly unhappy to find her there, alone in Reed's office. Greg Saucier had gone out on patrol, but even he and the other officer, Pete Rasinski, returned to clock out for the day.

The sun was well on the way to setting when Brie gave up and left. Before going back to Aunt Marilyn's, she wanted to pay her mother's grave another visit.

As before, the small cemetery looked peaceful. Brie parked her car, making her way unerringly toward the massive oak tree. As she neared the tombstone, the bright splash of color at the base of her mother's tombstone made her pause.

Blood-red roses. Someone had placed an enormous bouquet of flowers at the base of the stone. And a note, she saw as she got closer. The folded piece of paper had been tucked in under the bow.

Gingerly, she worked the note free and opened it. *Don't worry, Elizabeth,* it said. *Your daughter will do what you could not. She will finally end our suffering and save us.*

The letter *e* was faint, at times entirely missing.

Heart pounding, Brie read it again. Her stalker—her

mother's stalker—was still writing notes to a woman long dead.

This made him crazier, and potentially more dangerous, than she'd originally thought.

Folding it carefully, her hands shaking, she caught herself wishing she knew where Reed lived. She needed to share this with him. But she didn't and she couldn't, so she drove back to her aunt's house, keeping an eye on her rearview mirror.

No one followed her. The stalker, whoever he might be, was biding his time.

Her aunt and uncle had left her a note. They'd gone bowling, which made Brie smile. Glad to be alone, she flipped on lights as she headed to her room, unwilling to let even empty rooms remain in darkness. Not this night.

Her bed looked so welcoming she nearly yanked back the comforter and climbed in. The events of the day—the bell, her panic attack, the headlong rush in the rain through the woods, the wolf and, finally, being shot at, made her want to curl up into a ball and sleep.

Instead, she grabbed a pad of paper from the desk. Time to make a list of questions she wanted answered. This entire secrecy thing felt like something out of the *Twilight Zone.* So far there'd been a curse and a bell and something called *change* that no one wanted to explain.

This was getting ridiculous. She'd been in Leaning Tree a few days. Instead of getting answers to her mother's death, flushing out the killer and then settling down to a nice, quiet life here, things had gotten worse. Had she really thought it would be easy?

Not only had she gained a stalker, but she'd had a man run away after he kissed her. The fact that man was the town police chief—excuse her, the *cursed* town police chief—didn't make things any better.

She was no closer to learning who'd killed her mother than she'd been when she arrived.

Focus on the positive. Chin on her hand, she toyed with the pen and began another list.

She loved it here. Leaning Tree had quickly become her home. She was sure now she belonged. So certain in fact, she'd been thinking of scouring the real estate listings in the *Leaning Tree Courier* for a place of her own. She wanted a porch and a yard and maybe a cat. With all the money she'd made selling the house in Boulder, she wouldn't have any difficulties paying cash for a home here.

But when she finally climbed into bed, she fell asleep thinking about Reed rather than her own problems.

In the morning, she woke to an empty house, though there was a pot of fresh coffee in the kitchen. She'd overslept, and not only had Uncle Albert gone to work, but her aunt had already left for her various charity projects.

Despite the kiss and its disastrous results, Brie knew she had to show Reed the note. Plus, she'd like to take another look at those old case files on her mother.

Still, before she left she went to look at herself in the mirror. Calling herself names, she ran a tube of lip gloss over her mouth. Car keys in hand, she fluffed her hair, made a face at herself and opened the front door.

A huge bouquet of flowers sat on the front porch.

Red roses—exactly like the ones she'd found yesterday, decorating her mother's grave. Tucked in the arrangement was a bulky envelope with her name written across the front in bold, red script.

Oh, geez. Brie jumped back, inside the shelter of the door frame. He'd come to her aunt's house after her. Her simple presence here could now potentially endanger her newfound family.

Chapter 8

Heart pounding, she looked left down the street, then right. She saw no one. Again she glanced at the roses. The lumpy shape of the envelope told her more than a simple card was inside.

What now? A gift from her stalker. Great.

Leaving the flowers on the front porch, she slammed the door shut and slid the dead bolt into place. Then she picked up the phone and called the police department, asking for Reed.

Ten minutes later, he pulled into the driveway.

She waited just inside the door, battling an absurd wish to fling herself into his arms.

"Hey." His dark gaze searched her face, before dropping to the flowers. She felt a shiver at the contact, even if it hadn't been physical. "Flowers, huh?"

"They were here when I opened the door this morning. I haven't touched them." She told him about the other roses she'd found at the cemetery, and then showed him the note that had been left on her mother's grave.

"Not good." He shook his head. Then, slipping on black gloves, he reached into the roses and picked the envelope up by one corner. He raised it to eye level.

Watching, Brie could've sworn he sniffed it before he took it down the porch steps and carried it over to the hood of his vehicle.

With one swift, savage motion, he ripped the thing open and shook the contents into his hand.

She moved closer to see, careful not to let her body touch his. "What is it?"

"A letter and this." In the palm of his hand he held an unidentifiable, shriveled, brown object.

"Oh." She swallowed. "Tell me that's not an animal body part."

"It's a wolf paw, complete with claws."

Brie recoiled, trying not to gag. "Why? Because I chased that wolf cub yesterday? Is this from the same person who was shooting? I don't understand."

"He's trying to tell you something." He held up the letter. Expression grim, he unfolded the paper. "'You'll make your mother proud.'"

"Just like the one on the grave. Like I'm to be some savior or something."

"Same typeface, too. Just like the one you got on your car. This and the token amount to a threat, even if it's not specific."

Bile rose in her throat. "He's skipping several steps," she whispered. "And I've done nothing to set him off. According to all the research I've done, I should still be getting nice letters."

Carefully he placed the envelope on the front seat of his pickup. "I'll take this with me. I want to send it to the lab to be analyzed, along with both of the notes."

"Is there anything I can do? I'd rather be proactive than reactive."

He gave her a wary smile. "We need to talk." He glanced down her aunt and uncle's quiet, tree-lined street. His professional expression and kind tone irritated her.

As though the kiss which had so disturbed her had never happened.

Part of her wished he'd yank her against him and kiss her again. Kiss her until they both were senseless, distracting her from this mess with the sensual comfort of his hard body.

But this was the real world, not fantasy.

She motioned him in and after closing the door and leaving the roses outside, she led the way to the kitchen. Without asking, she poured him a cup of coffee.

Reed drank deeply, then set the cup down. He met her gaze, his expression serious. "The stalker sending you a wolf paw has me worried. He's raising the stakes, too soon. This leads me to believe he might make a move a lot earlier than I figured."

"That occurred to me, too." She looked around her aunt's tidy kitchen. "I don't feel safe now, not even here. And my aunt and uncle… I don't want to endanger them. Maybe I should move back to the motel."

"Bad idea. The motel's even worse. More anonymous, easier for him to get to you. Until we figure this thing out, you really need a round-the-clock guard."

"So give me one."

"I would if I could. But I have a small department, you've seen it. There are just me and two officers. I can't spare the men."

She set down her coffee cup. "What are you saying?"

"I want to make sure you're protected. You going to the motel will make that damn near impossible."

Lifting her chin, she stared at him. "I refuse to put my aunt and uncle in danger."

"Have you told them about the stalker?"

"No. I haven't discussed that with anyone, besides you. I can't— I don't want to worry them."

"Believe it or not, your aunt Marilyn can take care of herself."

"She's an older woman. This stalker could hurt her. He killed my mother. I won't risk it." To hide her agitation, she got up and refilled their cups. Keeping her back to him while she added cream and sugar, she tried to think of another plan.

Reed beat her to it. "You can stay with me. I have an extra bedroom. That way, I could keep an eye on you at all times"

She nearly choked on her coffee. "What did you say?"

He shrugged. "Stay at my place. I've got space. My room's on the other side of the house from the guest bedroom, so you'd have total privacy."

Good Lord. Her entire body went warm at the thought. That alone told her this was a terrible idea. "Wouldn't that be taking your job a bit too seriously?"

"I don't think so." He shrugged again. "My job is protecting the citizens of Leaning Tree. I don't want you in danger."

"I barely know you. Or you me."

"So?" He shrugged. "I'm a police officer. That's what

I do. I can't protect you here, or in the motel if this stalker decides to become more aggressive."

Logic. Again. Perfectly, reasonable logic. How could she refute that? Yet she knew staying with Reed would bring nothing but trouble.

"What about the curse?" she blurted. "Surely if I stay with you, we run the risk of bringing down the curse."

He didn't even blink. "No, we don't. The curse only applies to women who have a relationship with Hunter men. We're not involved romantically."

Yet. Had she just thought that? She sure as hell hoped she hadn't said it out loud. A quick glance at Reed's impassive face told her she probably hadn't. He sipped his coffee, his gaze steady, waiting patiently for her answer.

Though gut instinct told her she should refuse him outright, what other options did she have? She couldn't endanger her new family. And the idea of staying alone in a motel creeped her out. Maybe Reed was right. Maybe they wouldn't get involved.

After all, he'd run away after kissing her.

Yet he *had* kissed her. And even now, she hungered for more. "How do I know you're not a wolf in sheep's clothing?"

He gave her a startled look, then laughed. "I won't seduce you. I can give you my word on that. Not with the curse hanging over me."

"You kissed me."

Compressing his lips into a narrow line, he looked down at his hands. "That was a mistake. It won't happen again. The only thing I care about is keeping you alive." He used his cop voice again.

She found herself oddly grateful. "Despite the

threat, I still want to find out the truth about my mother."

"With you safe, I'll be better able to focus on tracking down your stalker. And, staying with me would give you access to more information. I have a computer, you can use the Internet. Much of my work on this case will have to be after hours. You can help me with that."

She stared, her throat tight. "You'd be willing to do that for me? Why?"

"I like you. And I owe your mother a debt."

This tidbit of information took the sting out of hearing him say he liked her. At least he hadn't called her *nice.* "What kind of debt?"

"Elizabeth was good to me, after my mother died. She helped me, mentored me, taught me not to hide when the other kids called me names. I wasn't exactly popular around here after my brother's wife died."

"Because of the curse?"

His mouth twisted. "Yes. Some even blamed me after she died, saying her association with me had gotten her killed."

"But you were a young boy." She searched his face. "You didn't have that kind of a relationship. Befriending you hardly qualifies, does it?"

"I don't know. I suppose not. But I was only eight years old. I thought my connection with her had somehow doomed her."

"But you know better now?"

He didn't answer.

She longed to reach out and smooth the hair back from his face. To kiss away the frown lines that appeared on either side of his well-shaped mouth.

That would be the worst thing she could do. For either of them.

So she stood motionless, listening to the steady sound of her heart beating, aching.

Finally, Reed's expression cleared. He gave her a wry smile, the professional, law enforcement face back. "I'd better be going. Let me know what you decide to do."

"I'll think about it."

"Don't think about it too long. You never know when this guy's gonna step things up."

Following him toward the door, she felt a chill skitter down her spine.

He stopped, his hand on the doorknob. "I got a call from my uncle this morning. Malcolm says you paid him a visit yesterday. He said you had some kind of weird reaction when you touched the bell. Is that true?"

Even thinking of the bell made her stomach tumble. "The bell was beautiful," she said, honestly. "But I have panic attacks, Reed. They happen for no reason, at any time. I think touching that bell triggered one."

"I see." She saw pity in his eyes. "Panic attacks. I'm sorry."

Lifting her chin, she shrugged. "Do you mind if I stop by the station later? I'd like to take another look at those files."

"Why not now? You can ride over there with me. I'd like to get photocopies of both those notes."

"Sure." She grabbed her purse and went, locking the door behind her.

Once at the police station, Reed led her into the conference room. The files were still stacked on the table, exactly where they'd left them. He left her alone to study them, retreating to his office and closing the door.

The other two police officers, Greg and Peter, poked their heads in to say hello. Tammy even brought Brie a doughnut, left over from the dozen she'd bought that morning.

Finally, Brie settled down to read.

Two hours later, she stood and stretched. She'd discovered a few things in the folders she hadn't read, and wondered why Reed hadn't mentioned them. Chief among them was the forensic report. The local investigator had written Elizabeth Beswick had died of what appeared to be a self-inflicted gunshot wound, fired at point-blank range.

But what Brie found odd was that the bullet had been made of silver.

A silver bullet! Brie hadn't even known such a thing existed. Silver bullets reminded her of old, black-and-white movies, and werewolves.

Reading further, the notes had indicated these were not commonplace, but had to be specially made. The notetaker had not seemed to find the composition of the bullet unusual in any way. He'd been a local cop at the time. Brie made a note to find this guy and interview him.

She also wanted to mention this to Reed. All of her mother's friends, and enemies—Scott Wells and Eldon Brashear among them—had been interviewed after her mother's death. Nothing of note was discovered.

Finally finished, she went looking for Reed. He was still in his office, door open now, with the phone cradled against his chin while he dialed. He hung up when he saw her.

"What's up?"

His expression changed when she mentioned the silver bullet. "I'll look into that," he promised.

She had the strongest sense he knew more than he was saying.

"Do you need a ride back to your aunt's?"

She nodded. "I'd like to get my car and run some errands downtown. Do you have time?"

After a quick glance at his watch, he smiled. "Sure. It's just about lunchtime, too. I can pick something up on the way back and eat it while I work."

When they arrived back at the house, Reed parked and left the engine running. Brie lifted her hand in goodbye and started for the steps.

"Wait." An undercurrent of warning made the single word a command rather than a request.

She froze, turning slowly to watch Reed jog up to her side. "What's wrong?"

"What side is your room on?"

"That side." She pointed to the left side of the house. "That's my window!" Her curtains hung out the window, flapping in the breeze.

"Did you leave it open?"

"No, I didn't. Aunt Marilyn has been running the air-conditioning."

"Wait here." Moving cautiously, Reed slipped around to the left side of the house. When he returned a moment later, his expression was grim. "Looks like someone broke into the house. The window isn't open. It's shattered."

Heart pounding, she took a step forward. "Aunt Marilyn!"

"I checked. Her car's not in the garage." He touched her arm, making her shiver as the now-familiar jolt went through her. "Steady, Brie."

"I'm fine." She shook off his hand. "We need to go inside. See what's missing."

"No, *I* need to go inside. You wait here." He started forward. Ignoring his instructions, she followed, close on his heels.

The front door was unlocked. The handle turned easily.

"I locked it when I left."

"Shh." Holding up his hand, he stepped over the threshold. "If you insist on coming, stay close behind me."

This time, she followed orders.

The den looked exactly as it had when she'd left it. Nothing out of order, magazines still stacked neatly on the oak coffee table. They moved into the kitchen, and that room was the same—undisturbed.

"Which way's your room?"

Brie pointed. When Reed moved down the hall, she followed. He stopped at the doorway, making her have to duck under his arm to see.

Inside, rose petals were scattered everywhere. The broken stems had been tossed on the floor amid shards of glass from the busted window. The room looked as though a jilted lover had flown into a rage.

But the mess and the flowers weren't the worst of it. What gave Brie chills was the stuffed toy wolf on her bed, a jaunty pink bow around its neck.

Her stalker had made another statement.

"You're out of here." Reed herded her away from the room. "Not tonight, not tomorrow, now. You're moving to my place."

One look at the set of his mouth told her it'd be pointless to argue. She briefly toyed with the idea of checking back in to her motel, but vetoed it. That would make her too easy to find.

"Fine." Agitated, she combed her fingers through her

short hair. "I'll bring my stuff over to your place as soon as you let me in."

"I have an extra key back at the office. If you'll follow me there, I'll give it to you."

"I'll stop by there later. For now, I've got to go find Aunt Marilyn. I'm going to have to tell her the truth."

Reed backed his pickup out of the driveway and waited in the street for her to go. On Wednesdays, her aunt volunteered at the Leaning Tree library on Main Street, downtown. She drove there and, spotting Marilyn's pale blue Cadillac, parked in a space near it.

The older woman beamed and waved as Brie crossed the polished marble floor. She stood behind the checkout counter, sorting a stack of books into neat, smaller piles. Her smile disappeared as Brie got closer.

"What's wrong?" Marilyn's sharp gaze searched Brie's face. "Has something happened?"

"Yes. We need to talk. Can you take a break?"

"Of course I can. Wait here." She bustled off, conferring with another woman in a low voice, before returning. "Follow me. We can use one of the offices."

Once there, Brie closed the door. Once it clicked shut, she filled her aunt in, leaving nothing out.

"Elizabeth got letters, too?" Marilyn fumbled for the chair, face so pale her freckles stood out. She dropped her bulk into the seat, twisting her hands together in her lap. "Brie, I never knew. Why didn't your father ever tell me?"

Brie stared. "I don't think he knew, until later. What do you mean by *too*? Did you receive some as well?"

"Yes, but that was a long time ago." Marilyn went on to described verbiage so similar to the ones Brie's mother had received that a chill skittered down Brie's spine.

"Did the letter writer ever try to contact you or leave you gifts?"

"No. Nothing like that." Clearly upset, her aunt's mouth twisted. "The letters stopped once Albert and I married. That must have been about the time Elizabeth started getting them. Why didn't she ever tell me?"

"Did you mention yours to her?"

Guilt filled Marilyn's big, brown eyes. "No. I'm afraid I didn't take them seriously. I showed them to Albert, and he didn't seem concerned. They were more like fan letters, after all. Then we got so busy with the wedding and all, by the time I thought of them again, they'd stopped."

Taking a deep breath, Brie shook her head. "I'm afraid this stalker was connected to my mother's death."

Marilyn's gaze went wide. "But Elizabeth was…are you saying you think she was murdered?"

"Yes, I am." Brie knelt down in front of her aunt and took her hand in hers. "I don't have any proof, not yet. But I'm looking. Reed's helping me. My investigation might be why the stalker is after me."

"He's worried you'll find him out?"

"That's what I think. Either that, or he only targets Beswick women."

Marilyn didn't even smile at her joke. Leaning forward, she squeezed Brie's hand. "I'm going to have an alarm installed. I don't want you to worry about him breaking in again."

Now came the difficult part. Especially knowing how her aunt felt about Reed.

"You don't have to do that. I'm moving out. Today."

"Moving out? But where will you stay?"

Brie took a deep breath. "Police Chief Hunter wants

me to stay with him. He feels he can better protect me there."

"Absolutely not." Marilyn pushed her bulk to her feet, still gripping Brie's hand. "Honey, I know you're new in town and Reed's a handsome man. But if you move in with him, you'll be putting yourself in even greater danger. The curse is worse that anything a stalker could do, believe me."

Wisely, Brie refrained from commenting on what she thought of the curse. Instead, she set about trying to soothe her aunt's fears.

"I'll be staying in a guest bedroom, not in his. Aunt Marilyn, there's nothing between us. He's been helping me look through the case files on my mother's death, nothing more." True, except for the matter of the kiss. She wouldn't mention that either.

"I'd so much rather you stayed with us." Wringing her hands, Aunt Marilyn's lower lip trembled. "Though Albert would probably agree that Reed can do a better job of protecting you."

"I'd rather stay with you, but Albert is right. And Reed thinks he has a better chance of catching the guy if I stay with him."

Her aunt's eyes turned hard, the tears vanishing as if they'd never been. "You be careful of that boy. He might be police chief, but he's still cursed. Most people in town know enough to keep their daughters away from him."

Oh geez. Reed hadn't been exaggerating. Poor guy. Keeping her thoughts to herself, Brie nodded. "I'll be careful."

"I'm serious, Brie. The curse is real. His wife died a horrible death."

Despite herself, Brie's ears perked up at this bit of

information. She hadn't ever asked what had happened to Reed's wife.

Without waiting for her to ask, Aunt Marilyn continued. "She was shot and killed by a hunter who thought she was a deer, we think. When he saw what he'd done, he ran off and left Teresa in the woods to die a slow, horrible death."

Shot? Brie had an awful suspicion. "Was this anywhere near Eldon Brashear's place?"

"No." Her aunt gave her an odd look. "You haven't been back out that way again, have you?"

"No, I haven't. Once was enough for me." So Reed's wife had been shot. As had Brie's mother. She wondered if the weapon had been the same kind. They could tell by the bullet, couldn't they? "So where was she shot?"

"A meadow on the outskirts of town. It used to be a popular place for weddings and such."

Remembering her mother's file, Brie decided to ask. "Was Teresa killed by a silver bullet?"

Marilyn narrowed her eyes. "Of course."

Of course? "Why? Was she a werewolf?"

All the color drained from Marilyn's face. "I…"

"I was kidding." Brie finally took pity on her. "That's just what silver bullets make me think of. But since when do hunters use them?"

"They do around here." Marilyn clamped her mouth shut. "Go on, now. I'm of half a mind to call Reed and let him have an earful."

Brie wanted to press for more information, but judging by her aunt's set expression, wouldn't get far. Instead, she stood on tiptoe and kissed her cheek. "Please don't. He's just doing his job."

She snorted. "Like hell he is. I've seen the way that boy looks at you."

God help her, Brie felt warm inside at the thought. She wanted to know exactly what her aunt meant by that, but had enough sense to realize she'd be bringing on more trouble if she asked. "There's nothing between us," she reiterated firmly.

"I don't know…" Marilyn seemed to be wavering. "As long as you're not attracted to him, I suppose it'd be all right. He could protect you better than your uncle and I."

Though she hadn't said she wasn't attracted to Reed—*that* would be an outright lie—Brie nodded. "I don't see how I have a choice. I wouldn't be safe in a motel."

"No niece of mine is staying in a motel." Marilyn pulled her close and hugged her. "I want you to stay safe, Brie Beswick, er, I mean Danzinger. You only just came back to us. I don't want to lose you again."

Chapter 9

Reed was on his way out when Brie pulled up to the police station. She nearly collided with him at the front door. "Where are you going?"

"Hunting potential stalkers." He gave her a grim smile. "I'm working my way down the list of your mother's friends and acquaintances. Starting with her former boyfriend, Scott Wells."

She stepped forward, blocking his path. "I'd like to go."

Staring down into her eyes, he opened his mouth and then closed it. "Come on, then. It's not far."

He wasn't kidding. As they rounded the curve where she'd seen the wolf cub, Reed slowed.

"His driveway is right past here." Turning left into what amounted to not much more than a rutted, dirt track, he stopped. "Show me where you were."

"Where I saw the wolves?"

"And where you were shot at."

She glanced around, disoriented. "Over there, I think."

"Lead the way." He got out of the cab, crossing around to her side to open her door.

She hesitated at the edge of the trees. "I think I entered the woods here." Nervously, she glanced around. "Are you sure it's safe?"

"I called ahead and let Scott know I was coming. Now, where did the shots come from?"

Brie moved forward, crashing through the underbrush. Twigs snapped, leaves rustled. Finally she found the clearing she'd stopped in before. "Okay, the cub stopped here, then took off. The mother wolf and her other babies were up that rise. And I was over there." Pointing west, she took a step away from the hill where the wolves had been gathered. "So that means the shots came from that direction."

Reed nodded. Here in the shadows of the forest, he looked even more mysterious, more dangerous. Studying him, she felt a thrum of desire.

Somehow, without her saying a word, she must have communicated this to him. He turned and stared at her, his gaze going dark.

"Reed..." God help her, she even took a step toward him.

He turned away. "You can help me look for shell casings." His tone was professional, detached. She must have imagined the matching need she'd read in his eyes.

Clearing her throat, she tried to match his tone. "Shell casings?"

"Yes. Unless he picked them up, they should be around here somewhere. I'm pretty sure whoever shot out your rear window used a rifle."

They found a spot where the underbrush had been trampled. A broken branch here, a crushed sapling there.

Finally, Reed stopped and bent over, scooping something from the ground. "Bingo." He showed her several shell casings. "Twelve-gauge shotgun." He dropped them into his pocket then took her arm. "Come on. Now we go talk to Scott."

Back in the truck, they continued driving up the path, bouncing over ruts. The pickup even bottomed out a few times. It seemed to Brie they went deeper and deeper into a never-ending forest.

"I feel like we're in some foreign country." Staring around her at the untamed wilderness, Brie felt a familiar aching need to run into the shadows of the woods. Ever since she could remember, she'd craved the forests. She'd never understood why.

Maybe she had some ancestral memory of the Catskills.

Finally, they pulled up to a ramshackle, log cabin. The place had a vague air of neglect, as though it were only lived in seasonally.

"Are you sure he's here?"

"Oh, yeah." Reed pointed to a huge, military-looking, dark green vehicle parked in front of a three-sided shelter. "That's his Hummer."

As they approached the front door, it opened before they knocked.

"Afternoon, Scott."

"Hey, Reed. What brings you to my neck of the woods?" The man, tall and slender with coal-black hair and glasses, smiled warmly at them. As his gaze touched on Brie, his smile grew more intimate, as if they were old friends.

She had to rub her arms to dispel a shiver of fore-boding.

Reed performed quick introductions. "Scott, this is Brie Danzinger. Elizabeth Beswick's daughter."

Scott cupped her chin. "You certainly look like her." When he released her, she stepped back quickly, until she came up against Reed's hard chest.

"Don't touch me again."

He cocked his head, smile gone. "I apologize. I meant no harm."

"None taken." Squeezing her shoulder, Reed warned her to let him talk. "As I mentioned on the phone, I need to speak with you for a few minutes."

"Come in, come in." Leading the way into the cabin, he kept up a running patter, shooting sidelong glances at Brie. "Did Reed tell you I used to date your mother back in college? I even considered marrying her, before she met your father."

Brie exchanged a quick look with Reed. "Er, yes, he did. That's partly why we want to talk to you."

Indicating a worn couch, Scott took a seat in an over-stuffed chair, crossing his legs. He wore polyester slacks, and polished loafers with no socks. "How's your father doing? Did he come with you to visit?"

When she told him her father had passed away, he expressed sincere-sounding condolences. Finally, he asked again what had brought them here.

"Brie was shot at on your property the other day." Removing the shell casing from his shirt, Reed held it up. "This blew out her back window. Do you own a twelve-gauge rifle?"

Scott's mouth fell open. "That was *you?* Red car, in the rain?"

Wary, she nodded. "Why'd you shoot at me?"

"Hell hounds, I'm sorry. I was only trying to scare them. I'm an expert marksman, so if I'd wanted to hit you, I would have."

"Scare who?" Reed asked.

"I've been having a problem with trespassers. Kids, teenagers, I think." Scott gave Reed a sharp look. "They've been messing with me, writing threats in red paint on my barn and setting trees on fire. Just last week they killed a couple of wolf cubs and left them on my back porch. Natural wolves, not…" he paused and grimaced. "Anyway, when I saw you near the other bitch and her litter, I thought you were there to harm them."

Brie gasped.

"Exactly," Scott said, grimacing before he turned his attention to Reed. "I've filed two complaints with your office. Spoke to Greg Saucier both times. He said he'd look into it."

"I'll check with him."

Uncrossing his legs, Scott started to push himself to his feet, then apparently changed his mind. Instead, he leaned forward, hands on his knees, and stared hard at Brie. "Miss, I'm very sorry. I'd never have shot if I'd known it was you."

Brie wasn't sure she believed him.

Later, driving back to town, Reed was quiet. He'd delivered what was probably his standard lecture on gun use, after which Scott Wells had thanked him.

"While he's a bit strange, he seems like a nice enough guy," she finally ventured. "I don't think he's the stalker."

"First thing you learn in law enforcement is never to dismiss the nice guys. Then again, you could be right.

GET FREE BOOKS and a FREE GIFT WHEN YOU PLAY THE...

Lucky 7

SLOT MACHINE GAME!

Just scratch off the silver box with a coin. Then check below to see the gifts you get!

YES!

I have scratched off the silver box. Please send me the 2 free Silhouette Intimate Moments® books and gift for which I qualify. I understand I am under no obligation to purchase any books, as explained on the back of this card.

DETACH AND MAIL CARD TODAY!

340 SDL D73Q   **240 SDL EE2T**

FIRST NAME   LAST NAME

ADDRESS

APT.#   CITY

STATE/PROV.   ZIP/POSTAL CODE

7	7	7	**Worth TWO FREE BOOKS plus a BONUS Mystery Gift!**
🍒	🍒	🍒	**Worth TWO FREE BOOKS!**
♣	♣	♣	**Worth ONE FREE BOOK!**
🔔	🔔	🍒	**TRY AGAIN!**

www.eHarlequin.com

(S-IM-12/05)

The Silhouette Reader Service™ — Here's how it works:

Accepting your 2 free books and gift places you under no obligation to buy anything. You may keep the books and gift and return the shipping statement marked "cancel." If you do not cancel, about a month later we'll send you 4 additional books and bill you just $4.24 each in the U.S., or $4.99 each in Canada, plus 25¢ shipping & handling per book and applicable taxes if any.* That's the complete price and — compared to cover prices of $4.99 each in the U.S. and $5.99 each in Canada — it's quite a bargain! You may cancel at any time, but if you choose to continue, every month we'll send you 4 more books, which you may either purchase at the discount price or return to us and cancel your subscription.

*Terms and prices subject to change without notice. Sales tax applicable in N.Y. Canadian residents will be charged applicable provincial taxes and GST. Credit or debit balances in a customer's account(s) may be offset by any other outstanding balance owed by or to the customer.

BUSINESS REPLY MAIL
FIRST-CLASS MAIL   PERMIT NO. 717-003   BUFFALO, NY

POSTAGE WILL BE PAID BY ADDRESSEE

SILHOUETTE READER SERVICE
3010 WALDEN AVE
PO BOX 1867
BUFFALO NY 14240-9952

NO POSTAGE
NECESSARY
IF MAILED
IN THE
UNITED STATES

If offer card is missing write to: Silhouette Reader Service, 3010 Walden Ave., P.O. Box 1867, Buffalo NY 14240-1867

The stalker doesn't want to kill you, at least not yet, so he wouldn't shoot at you. Scott's story makes sense."

The *at least not yet* made her shiver. "I think you need to look at Eldon again."

"I will, though he's a bit too obvious in his dislike of you."

"Dislike?" She didn't believe him. "Don't you mean hatred?"

Reed sighed. "I'm keeping my eye on him, Brie. The stalker is probably someone we don't even know."

Once back at the police station, Brie refused Reed's offer of a key. "No, you can give that to me later. No way am I going to your house without you there. I need to run some errands, then I'll meet you at your place after dinner." With Tammy and Pete Rasinki watching curiously, she waved goodbye, then got in her car and drove downtown. Visiting her aunt at the library had given her an idea. She had a few things she wanted to research, such as the word *change* and silver bullets, to name just two. And she could look at old microfiche newspapers and read about her mother's death. Also, for good measure, she'd see what she could find out about this mysterious curse everyone talked about.

Brie had arranged to meet Reed at his place after supper. She'd already packed her suitcases and Aunt Marilyn had helped her load them in her trunk. She ate dinner in her car at the A&W stand, treating herself to a root beer float for dessert. Sometimes a girl just needed vanilla ice cream and root beer.

She'd learned nothing new at the library. She couldn't find any books on the Hunter family curse. And the newspaper clippings had confirmed what the police records showed—a thorough investigation had been made into her mother's death. No evidence of foul play had been found.

Putting it off as long as she could, she waited until the sun began to set. Finally, filled with a curious mixture of anticipation and nervousness, she headed toward Reed's house. He'd given her directions earlier and, knowing her propensity for getting lost, had even driven her by the place on the way back from Scott Wells's.

By the time she pulled into his driveway, dusk had fallen. The western sky was dusty rose, promising a scorching next day.

Parking, she sat in her car and stared at his residence. A small frame dwelling painted a soft cream color, yellow light beamed from the big picture window in the front, a welcoming sight. This was the kind of house she'd often dreamed of as a child, the sort of place it would be easy to call *home*. In the glow of twilight, she could easily imagine rosy-cheeked children tumbling over the plush lawn, with a tail-wagging golden retriever standing cheerful guard.

She blinked, chiding herself for her foolishness.

As she got out of her car, Reed opened the front door, bounding down the porch steps two at a time when she popped her trunk to get her suitcases. Glad of the distraction, she took a deep breath, knowing she didn't want him to see the raw emotion that surely shone from her eyes.

"Here, let me help you." His deep voice had her nerve ends thrumming. Reaching around her, he hefted the larger of her two bags. "You want to hand me the other?"

"I can get it." Steadying herself, she lifted the duffel

bag and slammed her trunk closed. Unable to resist, she glanced at his house once more, again struck by a sense of wonder, her chest tightening. How on earth would she be able to do this, especially when a simple look at his home made her want to cry?

"Are you all right?" Halfway up the steps, Reed paused, his dark gaze searching her face.

"I'm fine." Having said that, she took a deep breath and steeled herself and followed him into his house.

The place even smelled like him. Masculine, and more achingly familiar than her short association with him warranted. She sniffed. "Hamburgers and fries?" Even though she'd already eaten, Brie's mouth began to water. "I didn't know you cooked."

He grinned, making her insides do cartwheels. "I make a mean burger. I just finished eating, but have plenty of meat. Would you like one?"

Tempted, despite herself, she peered up at him, then shook her head. "No thanks, I'd better not. I ate earlier at the root beer place."

"Suit yourself." Hefting her suitcase effortlessly, he started down a narrow hallway. "Your room's this way."

She stood in the doorway and stared. Painted in a soft sage, the green and gold comforter and floral prints had an overall restful effect. About to ask if he'd decorated the room himself, she nearly kicked herself. His deceased wife had most likely done it.

"I'll let you get settled." The perfect host, Reed brushed past her, sending a tingle to her toes. He disappeared down the hall, leaving her alone, full of so many conflicting emotions, she couldn't breathe.

Panic attack? She stood stock still, concentrating on her heartbeat, willing herself to calm.

As swiftly as the unsteadying feeling began, it passed. Not a panic attack then. Just nerves.

After depositing the duffel on the bed next to her suitcase, Brie dusted her hands off on the front of her jeans. It was a pleasant room, a wonderful house. She would be safe here, however temporarily. She couldn't have asked for anything more.

Still, she felt vaguely uncomfortable, restless. More than anything she longed to walk outside, even in the darkness. She wanted to slip under the trees, take shelter in the woods. If Reed would go with her, she'd be safe.

Heading in the direction he'd gone, she went to look for him. But she encountered only a deserted kitchen, den and dining area. Ditto for the back patio. Reed was nowhere to be found. One door, most likely to his bedroom, was closed. Was he in there? Should she knock?

Though she felt like a big coward, she decided against being *that* proactive.

Glancing at the clock, she thought maybe she could go to bed early. She needed the rest—if she could sleep. And that was a big *if*.

Outside, crickets chirped. The sounds of summer made her ache again, longing for an indefinable something.

Once in her room, she turned down the covers, plumped the pillow, and clicked off the light before changing into her boxer shorts and cami. Then she climbed between the sheets and closed her eyes, praying for sleep.

Reed heard Brie puttering around his house and stayed in his room. He wanted her so badly he shook. He, the consummate cop, didn't trust himself around her. If she brushed up against him, even once, he knew his limited control would snap and he'd take her mouth in a savage kiss, like he had once before. Only this time, he wasn't sure he'd be able to stop.

Just thinking of her soft, pliant body pressed to his made him groan. Thankfully, her room was on the other side of the house, so he wasn't tortured by the sounds of her getting ready for bed. Bad enough that the peach scent of her already permeated every corner of his home.

Restless, he paced the twelve by eleven outline of his bedroom, and cursed his need. He had to get a better grip on his self-control. And he knew exactly how to do that—go into the forest and change. Otherwise, this would be a long, long night.

He waited until the total absence of any sound told him she'd gone to bed. Then, barefoot and wearing only boxers, he padded into the kitchen, heading for the back door. A squeak of the floorboards warned him.

"Reed? Can I go with you?"

"Huh?" One hand on the doorknob, he froze. Too late, he smelled peaches. "Why aren't you asleep?" He turned to look at her, his first mistake.

"I couldn't sleep." She came closer, near enough for him to note the hollow at the base of her throat, where her pulse beat. Damn it. If he reached out his hand, he could stroke her soft skin. His blood boiled.

"I feel unsettled, on edge." She licked her lips, an unconscious gesture which sent heat straight to Reed's groin.

He groaned under his breath.

"Reed?" She took another step.

Clenching his jaw, he inhaled a shuddering breath and held his ground. He couldn't help but marvel that he, police chief of Leaning Tree, was more afraid of facing Brie in his own kitchen than of any hardened criminal he might meet in a dark alley.

Stupid. Dangerous.

Yet he couldn't stop his hungry gaze from roaming over her. She wore a lace-strapped T-shirt and hip-hugging shorts that fit her like a glove. Her pale legs looked impossibly long, and despite her words to the contrary, her heavy-lidded eyes and mussed hair told him she'd slept, even if only for a short while.

Brie. Unknowing, she'd wrapped herself around his bones, snuck into his soul. His body recognized her for what she was—or what she could be, were he not cursed. His mate. Brie.

Not possible, not for him. Not ever for him.

Damn, damn, damn.

She moved closer. "What's wrong?"

Mouth dry, Reed started to shake. He wanted her more than he'd ever wanted a woman. And knew he could never, ever have her.

"Can I go with you?" she repeated, her lovely eyes wide and innocent. Then, hounds help him, she reached out and touched his arm. He shuddered.

"What?"

"Can I go with you? Out there. I need to walk in the trees." She came even closer, apparently having no idea how much danger she was putting herself in. So close, her breath tickled his bare chest, making his nipples harden.

Reed had nowhere to retreat except outside. "No," he ground out. Then when her face fell, he shook his head, trying to clear it. "Brie, I'm sorry, but I need to be alone."

"But—"

"No. Seriously." He managed to get the words out while he yanked open the back door. "Stay here."

He didn't wait to see if she listened.

Still, to give himself credit, this time, he didn't run. He would not make her think she repulsed him, like the last time, when he'd kissed her.

Besides that, he was older. The police chief. Control was his middle name.

He didn't look back. When he finally slipped into the dark woods, he let his breath out in relief.

Control was his middle name? He snorted. When had he started lying to himself?

He pulled off his boxers, hanging them over a low tree branch. Aroused and aching. Stupid, stupid, stupid. With a burst of frustrated anger, he closed his eyes and began the change.

In a moment, he was his other self. Pack. Wolf. Fierce and strong. And finally, free. Human lust and confusion were more simple urges now. He would run and he would hunt.

He lost himself to the solid feel of the earth under his paws as he ran.

Later, much later, Reed changed back, feeling as he always did, sore and older and...more sane. He stepped into his shorts and ran a hand through his hair. Though he'd chased a rabbit or two for fun, this run had been bloodless. He'd known, even as a wolf, he couldn't go home with blood on his hands and face. If Brie had waited up for him, that would be disastrous.

Waited up for him. Struck by the phrase, he exhaled. It had such an intimate sound to it. Thinking of her in her soft pajamas sent a tremor through him. Though he wanted her, he had to force himself to consider reality. He was cursed. With each step he took toward home, he reminded himself of the reasons why he couldn't have a relationship with Brie. His mother, brother and sister-in-law and, finally, his wife. He had vivid memories of how the bell had rung, solid and unbroken on his wedding day three years ago, when he and Teresa, newly married, had laughed off any thoughts of the curse.

One year later, she was dead.

With each painful memory, his resolve strengthened. As long as he could remind himself of this black blot upon his soul, resisting Brie should be much easier.

Slipping in the back door, he found the kitchen empty, though she'd left the light on over the sink. Both relieved and disappointed, he went to the fridge and poured a glass of cold milk.

On the way to his bed, he passed Brie's room. She'd left her door cracked. Despite his best intentions, he stopped and inhaled. Peach-scented lotion. Brie. Longing slammed into him with the force of a hurricane. He shook his head and called himself a fool.

Forcing himself to continue down the hall, briefly contemplating exchanging the milk for whiskey, he entered his room and locked the door. Though he'd exhausted his body, he knew sleep would not come easily.

The next morning, the wonderful and homey scent of maple-flavored bacon and fresh coffee woke him. Stretching, he swung his legs out of the bed, relishing the familiar ache of his overused muscles. Somehow, he'd slept, and deeply. From the instant he'd laid his head on the pillow until now, he remembered nothing.

With the bright summer sun shining in through his

window, he pulled on a shirt and tattered cut-offs and followed his nose down to the kitchen.

When he got there, he stopped in the doorway, struck by the scene in front of him. With her back to him, Brie stood at the stove, flipping bacon. She had the radio on low, top-forty stuff with a lively beat. Unaware of his presence, she sang along to the music, occasionally sashaying her hips and kicking up her foot behind her.

He felt his heart kick, then resume the normal beat, slow and steady in his chest. Unable to keep from letting his gaze roam over her, he drank in the sight of her, aching from need, from longing, yet happier than he'd been in months.

The cooking food drowned out the ever-tantalizing scent of her peach lotion, for which Reed was both grateful and disappointed.

"Good morning," she said, without turning.

He mumbled a reply in kind, snagged a mug and filled it with coffee, before dropping into a chair.

"Hungry?" She turned to look at him, her eyes bright and very blue. Another man might drown in those eyes. Not him. Starting to shake his head, he realized she'd asked him a question.

Jaw clenched, he nodded. "You didn't have to cook. I always do for myself." If she saw what he normally ate for breakfast, she'd probably be shocked. A bowl of raisin bran went a long way on a harried morning.

"I know." Her smile didn't waver. "But I was hungry and, since I haven't had a chance to go to the grocery store, I thought this was the least I could do. I will be eating your food, after all." With a graceful movement, she swung around and placed a heaping platter of bacon on the table.

Ravenous, he resisted the urge to scarf down the entire rasher.

The song on the radio changed to a romantic ballad. Something about losing love forever. Just what he needed to hear to remind him.

"So, about last night." She pulled out a chair across from him and bounced in to it.

Reed froze. On his third piece of bacon, he chewed, swallowed and managed a casual nod. "What about it?"

"You went into the woods in the middle of the night."

If she wasn't going to eat the bacon, he was. He reached for another couple of pieces. "So?"

"You were gone a couple of hours."

Chewing, he raised a brow. "And?"

She pushed the plate of bacon over to him. "Did you go into the woods to change?"

Chapter 10

He nearly choked on his bacon. Grabbing his mug, he gulped scalding coffee to clear his throat.

Unfazed, she simply waited.

Did she really know? If so, who had told her? What did she think? Most importantly, was she aware she herself had the capability to become a wolf?

Cautiously, he pushed back his chair and went for a coffee refill. Stalling, yes, but he didn't want her to see his face until he could find the perfect words.

"You know?" Turning, he kept his expression neutral.

"I know," she said. "You don't have to pretend any longer."

Something about the way she watched him, eyes a little too wide-open, mouth curved in a pleasant, calm smile, set off an alarm. Did she really know, or was she bluffing?

Taking his time, he avoided speaking until he'd settled back in his chair. "You're not shocked?"

Her gaze flew to his, surprised. But he saw no fear in her. "No." She licked her lips.

"Not horrified? I'd be pretty stunned, if I found out something like this."

She opened her eyes even wider, if possible. "Of course not. Why would I be horrified?"

Of course not? "You know nothing." He kept his tone flat, nonaccusatory. "You're on a fishing expedition, trying to see what you can find out."

"Okay, so you got me. I don't really know." Blowing her breath out in a frustrated puff, she ran a hand through her hair, mussing it sexily. "But I'd like to. Why won't anyone tell me anything? Everyone keeps skirting around the issue, hemming and hawing whenever I ask."

With narrowed eyes, he watched her and said nothing.

"I trust you, Reed." She leaned close, sending a hint of peaches his way. "You've always been straight with me. So I'm asking you. Please. Tell me about this changing thing."

He swallowed, his heart a trip-hammer in his chest.

"You may be right," he said slowly. "I don't see the point in continuing to try and hide the truth." Hell, Leaning Tree was an entire town of shape-shifters and, innocent or not, she was one of them now. Even if she hadn't yet changed.

"Then tell me."

He sighed. "Maybe you're right. Maybe it is time. Show me your allergy medicine."

Rearing back in her seat, her eyes narrowed. "What?"

"If you want answers, humor me. Go get your allergy medicine. I need to see what you're taking."

Silently she rose and left the room. A moment later, a small blue and white box in hand, she returned. "Here." She tossed it on the table. "Over the counter stuff. Not even prescription. You've mentioned this before. What does this have to do with anything?"

He turned the box over, reading the ingredients out loud. "Here we are. Pseudophrine hydrochloride."

"And?"

Placing the box on the table between them, he looked her full in the face. "This drug suppresses change."

"There's that word again. Explain *change*. What's it mean?"

He leaned back in his chair while he searched for the right words. Though he'd done his fair share of mentoring Pack youth, he'd never acted as a Nya. And he'd never tried to explain what being a shifter meant, what the Pack was, to an outsider.

This was Brie. She wasn't an outsider. Not really. She was one of them. He needed to remember that.

"I'm going to start with the past. Your parents. Your father was human. Your mother…"

Silently, she waited. He had a sense she was holding her breath.

"Your mother was a shape-shifter. Most of this town is. We call ourselves the Pack."

Nothing registered on her expressive face. Not shock, not surprise, not disbelief. She'd heard his words, but she didn't understand them. "A shape-shifter? What?"

"We change into wolves." He tried again. "And because you are half-shifter, your blood also gives you this ability. That's why your father gave you that allergy medication. You've taken those pills since you were a child, haven't you?"

"Allergy pills?" She looked at the box on the table, still unable to make the connection. "Yes. My father told me I'll always have to take them, every day."

"So you never have skipped a day?"

"I try not to." With a quick shake of her head, she leaned forward. "Come on, Reed. Get real. Shape-shifters? Allergy pills that do double duty? I ask you for answers, and you give me this garbage?"

He reached out and touched her arm. "I told you learning the truth would be rough."

"You haven't told me the truth."

"Brie, I'm not lying to you. This is what change means. We shift our shape into that of a wolf."

"That would explain the silver bullets," she said, almost to herself. "But honestly, this is unreal. Not only do I have some crazy stalker after me, but now this! Either I have to accept that I've stumbled into an entire town full of nutcases, or believe in werewolves."

Wincing at the hated word, he reached his other hand across the table for her, and stroked her arm. Her creamy skin felt soft and warm. Fleetingly he longed to go to her, to gather her close and hold her, murmuring soothing words of comfort. He wanted to lightly touch his mouth to the hollow of her throat, where her pulse jumped and leaped.

But he couldn't. He knew if he continued to touch her, the simple act of trying to provide comfort would spiral into something more.

Jumping up, she pushed away from the table. "Thanks." Anger made her voice shake. "You've single-handedly ruined every concept I had about you and this town."

Standing, he sighed. "I expected you to be furious. Listen Brie, you have a couple of options. You can go talk to your aunt Marilyn, or one of your cousins. Ask Father Malcolm. He's a priest, he can't lie. Tell them you know, tell them I told you. They'll corroborate what I've said."

Her eyes spat blue fury as she raked her gaze over him. "That's one option. What's the other?"

He pointed toward the woods. "We can go outside and I can show you. Once you see me change, you'll believe."

"Oh, no." Backing away from him, she made it to the door. "I'll take my chances with Aunt Marilyn. Then, if she doesn't agree with me that you have serious delusions, we'll talk."

She took off out the door before he could reply.

Driving, Brie kept her speed at the limit, no more. Even going thirty, she'd reach her aunt's neighborhood in ten minutes. She didn't call ahead, wondering if Reed would. She hoped not, as she'd prefer to have the element of surprise on her side.

Ringing the bell, she smiled through the necessary greetings, hugs and small talk. Only when Marilyn led her back to the kitchen, where a pot of stew meant for lunch bubbled on the stove, did Brie broach the subject.

"*Reed* told you this?" Aunt Marilyn's nostrils flared. "I'd like to have a chat with that boy."

Since the boy in question was a thirty-year-old man, Brie let that comment go. "All I want to know is if it's true."

Aunt Marilyn stared at her in silence. "Brie..."

Brie watched her closely. "You haven't denied it."

All at once the outrage seemed to leave Marilyn. With a sigh, she deflated. "I need to know something first, Brie. How long are you really staying here in Leaning Tree?"

"I was planning to stay here forever. I was hoping to buy a house."

"Then maybe Reed's right. You're family. You have a right to know your own potential."

She couldn't believe it. Swallowing, she stared. "Are you saying…?"

Marilyn nodded. "Reed told you the truth. We're all shape-shifters."

"Oh my God." Stunned, Brie gripped the kitchen counter. "You really think you're…werewolves?"

"Not think. We are. And we prefer the term *shifters*." Dropping her bulk into the nearest chair, the older woman reached for the phone. "Let me call Edie. She's closer to your age. Maybe she could explain things better."

"Edie? Edie's one, too?" Since her legs felt shaky, Brie too groped for a chair. "I'm finding this all very hard to accept."

"I know, dear." Dialing, Marilyn listened, then replaced the receiver without speaking. "No answer. She's not home. I didn't leave a message, so we'll try again later."

Restless, stunned, not sure what to think, Brie jumped to her feet. "I hope you don't mind if I pace. I can't…I feel…"

"Like your entire family's gone insane?" Humor rang in the older woman's voice. "Like maybe someone has been putting hallucinogenic drugs in the water supply?"

Brie gave her a reluctant smile. "Yes, that about sums it up."

"Mass delusion?" Aunt Marilyn laughed. "I can imagine what you must think, coming in from outside. It's got to be hard. First you learn you have an entire family you never knew about, and now you find out that same family imagines themselves to be shape-shifters."

"Not just my entire family. Apparently the entire town."

"True. How are you going to deal with that?"

"Deal with it?" Flabbergasted, Brie could barely speak. "I really don't know." Suddenly her aunt's small living room felt too confining. She stifled down her rising panic—she would not allow herself to have a friggin' panic attack. Not here, not now.

Still, the very act of breathing seemed a struggle. "I need to go outdoors."

"To the woods?"

Staring, her chest heaving, Brie nodded. "Maybe. When I go into the trees, I feel better. How'd you know?"

"That's what we all do, sweetheart. When we're confused, or angry, or simply need to think."

Oh God. Still fighting her rising panic, another thought occurred to her. "Is that where you go when you…er…?"

"Change? Yes."

That did it. Brie headed for the door. She wanted to pace, no—hell, she wanted to run. Until she could no longer feel the cold tendrils of panic clawing at her chest. It took every bit of willpower she possessed to keep herself from bolting out the door.

"You're shaking!"

"Sometimes, I get…" Unable to finish, Brie swallowed.

"Scared? Do you have panic attacks, honey?"

Brie froze. Swung around. "How did you know?"

"It's a side effect of denying your body the change. Once you accept this, and let yourself shift, they should stop."

Suddenly, absurdly near tears, Brie started moving again. "You're saying my father knew all this? That he lied to me? Because he was human, he didn't want me to change? To become a…"

"Yes. I'm sorry, Brie."

"That's just great. Simply wonderful. I'll tell you, I'm not sure what to think right now. I mean, who believes in werewolves?"

"Shifters." Aunt Marilyn followed her. "There's one way to settle all this, you know."

"Really?" She'd try anything at this point. Anything a little less…weird. "What's that?"

"Stop taking your allergy medication. One of the ingredients in it suppresses the ability to change. Give it a few days to get out of your system, and find out for yourself."

Now that was a novel idea. Why hadn't *she* thought of it? Skip a few days of allergy pills, go out into the woods and—then what?

Nothing. Nothing at all. When she didn't become a werewolf, would she be kicked out of town because she wasn't one of *them?*

"I'll think about that," she promised. Oddly enough, the panic attack which had been threatening, had disappeared. The power of suggestion?

"Come here and let me hug you."

Brie didn't hesitate. Crazy or not, this was still her aunt. Aunt Marilyn wrapped her close and squeezed. "Remember this, Brie. Right now you might think we're all insane, but we're still family and we love you."

With a lump in her throat, Brie nodded. "I've got to go."

"Where are you going?" Concern echoed in Marilyn's voice.

"I was thinking about the church. I like that place, and Father Malcolm's good to talk to."

Marilyn regarded her gravely. "Good idea. He might be able to help you come to grips with all this."

With a nod, Brie waved good-bye and climbed into her car. She drove off, feeling like she'd entered the twilight zone.

Good Lord, how'd she get into this mess? Maybe she needed to research mass hysteria. Maybe she— Brie slammed on her brakes as a rabbit darted in front of her car. Shaking, she pulled over to the side of the road as an even worse thought occurred to her.

Did this shared delusion have anything to do with her mother's death? And the Hunter family curse, with their unbreakable church bell? Weird as this sounded, were they all tied together, somehow?

Pulling back onto the road, she headed downtown. The church was exactly what she needed right now. Father Malcolm, with his soothing voice, reminded her of her father. And he was a priest—surely he didn't participate in this insanity. He was used to comforting people and offering advice. She'd go visit him, have a cup of coffee, confess her doubts and see what he had to say.

All the shops were open as she pulled onto Main Street. She checked her watch, barely 10:00 a.m. Later than she'd realized, this was the perfect time to stop by. Too late for breakfast, too early for lunch.

Letting herself in to the church, with the sun streaming multicolored through the stained glass windows, she waited for that sense of peace to steal over her. Instead, her heart continued to race, and she felt as though even a marathon run wouldn't calm her down.

Whether her aunt was correct or not, Brie needed to walk in the forest, but after what had happened last time when she'd seen the wolves, she wouldn't be caught dead near the trees.

Those wolves might have been her relatives.

Chagrined at her wayward thoughts, she grimaced. A wolf was only a wolf. There were no such things as werewolves or shape-shifters. Just because they all believed didn't mean she had to. She was a normal human woman. She refused to participate in their delusion.

Turning slowly, she took a deep breath and studied the small church's interior. Again she noted the wolf images in the stained glass and the wolf heads carved in the end of every pew.

If believing in werewolves was a mass delusion, apparently it had been going on a long time. What had Father Malcolm said when she'd asked him? *Wolves are our token animal. We are quite fond of them around here.*

She'd bet they were.

Her footsteps echoed in the absolute silence. Since Father Malcolm didn't materialize instantly, she walked to the back and chose a candle. Muttering her prayer, she lit the wick and dropped a dollar into the metal box.

"May all your prayers be answered."

Brie jumped. "Father Malcolm!" She forced her expression into a smile. "I hope I haven't come at a bad time…"

"Of course not." He cocked his head, studying her. "Are you all right? You look upset, ill-at-ease."

"I guess I am." She gave a grim nod. "Do you have a minute to talk?"

He took her arm. "Of course I do. Let's go into the back. I've got a fresh pot of coffee brewing, and Mrs. Maloney brought over a batch of her famous oatmeal cookies."

The scents assailed her nose the minute they entered his hallway. Homey scents. Comforting, like her aunt Marilyn's stew. Unexpected tears filled her eyes. She blinked them away.

As before, he poured them each a mug of coffee. Setting a platter of cookies on the table between them, he pulled out a chair and indicated she should do the same.

"Before we start," between lowered brows, he studied her. "Tell me this has nothing to do with my nephew."

His nephew? Ah, Reed. "In a way, it does."

He scowled. "That boy should know better. After what happened to his wife…"

It took her a moment to realize he meant the curse. "Oh, no. Nothing like that."

"I must confess, I am worried. I heard you and Reed were living together."

"Living together?" She straightened, suppressing the urge to rub her temples. Why hadn't she thought of how her sleeping arrangements would look to others? "Hardly. I'm staying at his house as a guest. In the guest bedroom."

Though the priest nodded, she sensed he didn't believe her. Right now, she didn't really care. She had worse things to deal with.

"There's a reason I'm staying with Reed. He's trying to protect me."

"Protect you? From what?"

"Someone is stalking me." Putting it so plainly, her words seemed out of place, as though saying them soiled the peace of the church.

Or else she had an overactive imagination.

"Stalking you? Why on earth would anyone want to do that?"

"I don't know." Feeling better, she sipped on her coffee and nibbled on a cookie. "Maybe because of my mother's death."

He opened his mouth, then closed it rapidly.

"And there's more." Brie reached for another cookie. "I've been asking questions about this change everyone keeps talking about. Reed finally told me, and my aunt Marilyn's confirmed what he said. So I came to ask you. What do you know about this werewolf thing?"

"Werewolf thing?" He laughed. "I thought you couldn't surprise me any more than you did a second ago, but I've never heard the Pack put quite like that." Still chuckling, he shook his head. "Werewolf thing indeed."

He'd said *the Pack*. Reed had used that term, too. Brie's stomach sank. "You buy into this fairy tale, too?"

"Child, it's not a matter of believing or not." Recovered now, he resumed his serene expression. "Like the curse, we simply *are*. There's little you can do about it."

Okaay. Fine. She shouldn't have expected Father Malcolm to be different. He believed wholeheartedly in the curse, after all. What was one more delusion?

She pushed herself to her feet. "I'm sorry. I've got to go. Coming here today was a mistake."

"Brie, please. Calm down. Let me help."

"Help?" She'd babbled on about werewolves and curses and he acted like they were real. He couldn't help. "I'm sorry, Father. I thought talking to you might be different. But you're no different than them."

"Neither are you." His calm smile told her he took no offense. "Once you accept that, you'll find peace."

Peace? "What are you all going to do when I prove you wrong? I'm going to try it, you know. Changing. And when nothing happens, what then? Are you all going to disown me, throw me out on my ear?"

He sighed. "So that's what this is all about. You're afraid."

"No fear." She raised her chin. "Can't you see how totally weird this is?"

"Of course I can." He patted the seat beside him. "Come sit. Let's talk about something else. We haven't talked too much about your mother."

If he'd wanted to distract her, that worked. Moving slowly, she lowered herself back in the chair. "I'd like that. You said you went to school with her. What was she like?"

"I promise I'll get those photo albums out one of these days. Your mother was special. She was a beautiful girl, an even lovelier woman." He gave a soft smile as he reminisced. "When she was pregnant with you, she positively glowed."

Eager to hear more, she kept still and silent.

"Everyone loved her. She had lots of friends." Lost in the past, he sipped his coffee. "She tutored Reed, did he tell you that?"

Brie shook her head.

"She had a way about her." He sighed. "She was the one who convinced me to enter the priesthood. Before her, I didn't think a shifter could ever serve the Lord."

That brought to mind another question. As long as she was playing along with this particular fantasy, she might as well ask. "Why? Why couldn't a, er, shifter work in the Church?"

He gave her a rueful smile. "Because I, like most of the general public, I suspect, found something dark and sinister about the entire concept. Humans becoming wolves? That didn't seem entirely angelic to me."

Taking a deep breath, she steeled up her courage. "I have to ask. Are they—you—shifters, I mean—evil?"

"Tied to the dark side?" Shaking his head, he wagged his finger at her. "Not at all. I must say, I find this conversation ironic. I'm trying to convince you the Pack isn't evil, as your own mother once convinced me."

"I never thought they were evil. I'm not entirely sure I believe in them, at all."

He chuckled. "Oh, Brie. You are like a breath of fresh air around here."

She let his comment go, not sure what to say. "Tell me more about my mother. What was she like? Quiet? Loud? Energetic? What were her hobbies?" Her father had spoken little of her mother. Even mentioning her name to Aunt Marilyn seemed to bring the woman pain. Brie was starving for information about the mother she'd never known.

Father Malcolm pinched the bridge of his nose again.

"She was so full of life and happiness, I found it difficult to believe she did what she did. That she could commit such an act, and take her own life…" His rich voice trailed off. In his tone, she heard a decades-old sorrow.

Hearing him, she felt a sense of loss so strong it might have been physical. "I don't believe she killed herself." She took a deep breath. "I think she was murdered."

"Nonsense," he said immediately. The certainty in his voice gave her pause. "Elizabeth took her own life."

"Did she talk to you?" Brie swallowed. "Before? In confession maybe? Is that why you can speak so definitely?"

His expression sad, Father Malcolm shook his head. "You know we priests are bound by an oath of silence. I cannot answer your question."

But his statement was answer enough. Her mother must have gone to him, confessed her sins—real or imaginary—and then…what? Committed suicide?

"If you knew, why didn't you stop her?" The words burst from her before she had time to consider them.

He turned his face away. "I didn't know she would do such a thing, Brie. I had no idea her light would so soon be extinguished."

Again, like when Aunt Marilyn spoke of her, Brie had the sense of fresh grief, as though twenty-plus years hadn't passed, as though her death had been yesterday.

"I'm sorry." Putting down her mug carefully, she stood. "I've got to go."

"I understand." Getting to his feet slowly, he nodded. "Go with God, my child."

Murmuring her thanks, Brie made her way from the room, muttering apologies all the way to the door.

A teenager with insolent eyes watched as she jogged to her car. A lit cigarette dangled from his mouth and, judging from his distance from the high school, he was skipping class. As Brie punched her remote and unlocked the doors, he came closer, staring at her with unabashed curiosity.

Not feeling safe—hell, even sixteen- or seventeen-year-olds can be stalkers—but refusing to give in to fear, Brie stared back.

He came around the front of the car to the driver's side, dropping his cigarette to the ground and grinding it under his heel, watching her intently all the while.

Jiggling her keys in her hand, she stared back. "Shouldn't you be in school?"

"Maybe." He shrugged. "You're the lady from Colorado, right?"

She nodded.

He took a deep breath, obviously screwing up his courage. "Can I ask you something?"

What now? Resigned, she nodded. "Go ahead."

"You're older than me, right?"

"Much older," she said, her dry tone wasted on him.

"That's what I thought. So how is it possible? I mean, I've heard, that is…"

"How is what possible? Spit it out."

"Is it true you haven't ever changed?" Coloring, he asked his question in a rush of words.

There it was again. *Change.* She was tired of hearing the word. "It's true." She made her voice cheerful, upbeat. "Not only haven't I done it, but I'm not sure I even accept such a thing as truth. So tell me, do you?"

Confusion danced across his youthful face. "Do I what?"

"Believe in werewolves? Have you changed yourself? Seriously?"

A look that could only be described as horror came into his face. "Uh, yes. I have." He backed away so fast, he stumbled. "Sounds like you need a Nya. And you're so old! I didn't believe when my friends told me about you…but now, I… Gotta go." He took off running, disappearing around a corner.

Watching him go, Brie shook her head. None of this made any sense. And now she had another word—Nya. Who knew what the heck that one meant?

Chapter 11

Sighing, Brie unlocked her car, climbed in and started the engine. Since the woods were off-limits, she'd drive around for awhile, and try to come to grips with all she'd learned.

Instead, she found herself at the library. She discovered a bunch of books on werewolves and a few more on town history. Carrying them to a table, she took a chair and began to read.

The sun was close to setting when she finally pulled onto Reed's street. Oddly enough, her quest for knowledge had turned up little to confirm his explanation. Other than mentioning wolves quite frequently, the town history books had made no mention of werewolves or any such thing. And the books she'd read on werewolves treated them as legend, as Brie had always believed.

Killing the engine, she sat in the car a moment to

gather her thoughts. Her life had changed a lot in a few short weeks. Standing still, it felt like the ground buckled beneath her. Now, she was about to take a big leap of faith and either prove the town right, or prove them wrong. She'd stop taking her allergy medicine and find out the truth once and for all.

Using the key Reed had given her, she let herself in. Reed was home, relaxing in a worn, overstuffed recliner. Had he mentioned this was his day off? She couldn't remember. He'd taken his shoes off and his legs were crossed at the ankles. His hands were behind his head. Instead of watching TV, he was listening to music. Ray Charles played low on the stereo—one of Brie's all-time favorite albums. She stopped short and faced him.

"Hi, there."

With a dip of his chin, he returned her greeting, pressing the remote to lower the stereo's volume. "I heard you went back to the church."

Small-town life. "Did your uncle call you?"

"No." He sat forward and ran a hand through his hair. His eyes were dark, his face shadowed. "Your aunt did. Are you all right?"

"I think so." Swallowing, she made a conscious effort to appear nonchalant. "Can we talk?"

"Sure." He motioned to the couch. "Have a seat. Would you like a glass of milk or cola or wine or something?"

"Wine sounds heavenly." Dropping her purse, she couldn't help admiring his backside as disappeared into the kitchen.

He returned with two glasses, setting them down on the coffee table. "So why'd you go see my uncle Malcolm?"

"I like him. We talked about my mother."

"They grew up together."

She sipped, watching him over the rim of her wineglass. "He mentioned she used to tutor you."

"She was my Nya."

"I heard that word earlier today. What's it mean?"

"Nya is like a mentor. In the Pack, every child has a Nya to help them through the first change."

She kept her face impassive. "I spent a couple of hours at the library, looking for more information, but couldn't find anything definitive."

"We have private libraries for that. The church has one. I've heard your aunt Marilyn has another."

"I see." She sighed. "Well, I've decided to give you people the benefit of the doubt. If you really think it'll work, I'm ready to stop taking my allergy meds. I'm going to try, but I might need a Nya myself. Obviously, I don't know how to change." Even saying the words felt silly.

Not to Reed, apparently. His eyes darkened. Slowly, he pulled his hands from behind his head, uncrossed his ankles and popped the recliner into an upright position. Though he leaned forward, he still seemed too far away, at least to her. She longed to go to him, to lean into him and rest her head on his shoulder.

"Once you stop taking it, the medicine will take a few days to work out of your system."

Her heart skipped a beat. "Then what?"

"Then we'll go to the woods." His smile looked both fierce and possessive. "I'd like to be your Nya, if you'll let me."

As her mother had been his. Assuming, Brie thought ruefully, she believed all this nonsense.

But what if it wasn't nonsense? What if, instead of a town-wide, mass delusion, this Pack really existed? If people truly could shape-shift into wolves, her entire perception of reality would be forever altered. She wasn't sure how she'd deal with that.

One day at a time, the way she'd managed her life thus far.

"So when do you want to do it?" She heard her own words and shook her head. "Teach me to change, I mean?"

"We'd better wait for next weekend. I want to take our time."

"Do I need to take a class or something?"

"The kids do. But you're older. You already understand the distinction between right and wrong, so I don't think you need to study. I'll tell you everything you need to know. How about Saturday morning, early?"

"Before breakfast?"

"Yes. Well-fed, your senses get a bit sated. I want you hungry. Aware."

An involuntary shiver went through her. Put that way, Reed made their plans sound sensual. She looked up and caught him watching her. "We don't need a full moon or anything?"

He laughed. "Urban legend. It's better in daylight. The forest is more…alive. Saturday morning it is."

Alive. Being so near to him, letting his deep voice roll over her, made her entire body feel alive. She struggled to focus.

"Will we—" she swallowed, trying to think "—run into anyone else? From town or anything?"

"No. Everyone pretty much stays on their own property, unless invited. We put a high value on privacy here."

She thought of the family picnic. "Those men who disappeared into the woods? They were together?"

"We're Pack. Often we like to change and run as a pack. Picnics, social gatherings, holidays—they're all good occasions for that." His smile was gentle. "But don't worry. No one will bother us. No one else will see."

"That works for me," she said, wishing he'd touch her, praying her longing didn't show.

"Perfect." Rising from his chair, he held out his hand. "It's a date."

She eyed him. Then, with a sigh, she pushed herself from the couch to meet him halfway. Sliding her fingers into his brought her jumbled feelings to the surface again. There it was again—that zing, that sense of connection, of mutual need and desire. An image flashed into her mind and she saw herself kissing him, running her hand down the plane of his flat stomach, the ridge of his hips, and farther.

Muttering an oath, he jerked his hand free. Somehow she knew his heart pounded as hard as hers. She stared. He stared back, his gaze dark and smoky. He felt it as strongly as she did. What was it with them—was her attraction to him due to the lure of forbidden fruit?

"Don't say that." His voice rumbled, a low growl that made her think of wolves.

Again, she hadn't been aware of speaking out loud. "I can't even touch you. Or you me. We're like matches and gasoline."

"I know." Raw need blazed in his face. "Even something stupid like shaking your hand makes me picture you naked, trapped underneath my body."

Her breath caught. Hell, she couldn't breathe. Retreat, her inner voice urged, sounding hollow in her ears. Do. It. Now.

"Do it now?" He cocked his head.

"Okay, stop that. I *know* I didn't say that out loud."

"You didn't?"

"No." Glad of the distraction, she took a step back. "If you tell me you're able to read my mind…"

"I can't. Though sometimes, I hear your thoughts."

"Hear my—" She bit her lip. What was one more oddity in a life that kept getting weirder and weirder. She looked at him, and the need returned, full force. "I was thinking I needed to run away." Yet she stood rooted in place, unable to move.

"That's a good idea, running away." Instead of taking his own advice, he moved, desire blazing from his eyes. "Because if you don't, I'm going to kiss you. And if I kiss you—"

"Who knows where that might lead," she finished for him. She went to move her feet and found she'd gone in the wrong direction. Toward him, rather than away. "Reed…"

"Hell hounds, Brie." He crushed her to him, claiming her mouth. She met him halfway, feeling like she could devour him. Hungry. So hungry.

"Starving," he agreed against her lips, before kissing her again.

Ah, damn. Drowning in sensation, her knees buckled. His arousal, strong and fierce, pressed against her belly, where her simmering desire blazed into an all-consuming need. If he so much as asked, she'd rip off her clothes right there, right then, and climb on top of him.

As she contemplated doing just that, the bay window behind the couch exploded in a shower of glass.

"Get down," Reed shouted, following the order up by pushing her to the floor. Shards of glass rained over them. He covered her with his body, only for an instant, before getting to his knees and moving quickly across the floor.

Dazed, she watched him go, only registering the danger when he returned from the kitchen with his gun drawn.

Reed heard the screech of tires and the roar of a gunned engine as a vehicle sped off down the street.

He ran to the front door and yanked it open. Too late. The shooter had gone.

And left a gift on the doorstep. A cardboard box, decorated with a bright pink bow. This time, there was no note.

Half-closing the door behind him so Brie wouldn't see, Reed opened the lid. Inside were bones and an animal's skull. Reed knew without a doubt once the lab had finished with the skeleton, it would be found to belong to a wolf.

He brought the box inside, knowing Brie would have to be told about this latest "gift." Glass crunching under his feet, he went to her. "Are you all right?"

She stared up at him in horror. "You're bleeding."

Too late, he realized he'd cut up his feet. His white socks were covered in streaks of blood, as was his carpet.

He swore. "I forgot I'd taken my shoes off."

"Stay still. Let me get some towels so we can clean you up." Brie pushed herself up off the floor, shaking off pieces of glass as she moved. When she returned with a wet washcloth and a big, fluffy towel, he let her push him back onto the couch. As she gently peeled off his now-blood-soaked socks and began picking glass shards from his feet, he set his jaw and said nothing.

"There." She blotted them dry. "They're still bleeding a little."

"Thanks." His simmering anger kept him from acting on his impulse to kiss her. Instead, he indicated his shoes. "Could you toss me those?"

"Sure, but your feet—"

"Are fine. Or will be. We shifters heal fast."

With a sigh, she crunched over and retrieved his shoes, handing them to him and watching while he slipped them on his feet.

"I can't believe someone shot at me *here*."

He gave her a dark look, so she'd see how much that infuriated him. "Someone shot at *us*—in *my home*. You're under my protection now. Whoever is doing this has just made a personal declaration of war."

She opened her mouth, but whatever she was about to say was cut off as a middle-aged man poked his head in the door. "Everyone all right in here?"

"We're fine, Justin." Reed pushed himself to his feet. "Whoever did this only got my window."

Outside, he could hear more voices. He quickly shepherded Justin back outside, so he could deal with the other neighbors' inevitable questions.

Sure enough, they'd emerged from the safety of their homes and were gathering in his front yard. Talking excitedly, all at once, Reed quickly learned they had no useful information. No one had noticed the color or make of the vehicle. They all reported hearing a gunshot, then the car taking off. By the time they ran to their windows and doors, the vehicle had roared off.

Damn it.

A police car pulled up. Greg Saucier, responding to a 911 call by a neighbor. Reed ordered the patrolman to search the neighborhood, saying he'd file the report on the window himself. Right now he had to handle damage control—the rest of the street had clustered three houses down, gaping at his house and closest neighbors. The gossip must be flying fast and furious.

Moving briskly, he headed over there. As soon as he approached, they fell silent. Finally, the woman from the cul-de-sac at the end of the street, Jeannie Roundhouse, stepped forward, electing herself unofficial spokesperson for the group.

"Was that a shooting?"

"Yes, ma'am." Putting on his most official face, he studied each face in turn. "They hit my front window, that's all. I've got an officer on it now."

Rather than placating her, his words seemed to make her curious. Jeannie's nostrils flared as if she scented more. "This is because of that woman, isn't it?" She pointed an accusatory finger at Brie, who'd come outside and watched from his front porch.

Before Reed could answer, Lilabeth Idell, Jeannie's best friend, chimed in. "And the curse. *Your* curse. Shame on you, Reed Hunter. Bringing down that curse on that poor woman. How could you do such a thing?"

He sighed, loud enough for them all to hear. "This has nothing to do with the curse."

"Then what?" They all began talking at once. He caught bits and pieces of each individual voice, words like *gangs* and *council* and *trust*.

Again he waited until the uproar died down. "I'm not sure why anyone wanted to shoot out my front window, but believe me, I intend to find out."

"This was a quiet street," Jeannie cried. Several others echoed her sentiment. "I've lived here twenty-four years and nothing like this has ever happened. We all had misgivings when you and Teresa bought that house, and thought for sure you'd sell once she died. I think you should move, Reed Hunter. I want to know I can still consider myself safe if I walk down the street."

Searching all of their faces, Reed wasn't surprised to note most of them wouldn't meet his gaze. Though he was used to such blatant prejudice, it never ceased to hurt.

Since the most exercise Jeannie got was walking to her mailbox, Reed doubted she'd need to be concerned. He kept his tone professional, as though her harsh words hadn't affected him. "Until I know more, I'll have to advise you to stay inside. Once I determine a motive, or a suspect, I'll be able to tell you more."

"Stay inside?" Samuel K. Cassin stepped forward, puffing his barrel chest out. "You know as well as we do that we can't do that. We all have to change, my man. And no one is going to make me give that up. No one."

Again the small crowd started talking, their voices more strident. This time, Reed didn't wait for them to fall silent. He raised his hand and said one word. "Enough."

Instantly silenced, they stared at him, some with hostility, others with curiosity shining in their eyes. "I've given you my best advice. Whether you choose to take it or not is up to you. I'm going to go back to my house, get the glass cleaned up and the window repaired and get to work finding out who did this." He turned on his heel and marched off, leaving them silently watching.

An hour later, a truck from the glass shop pulled up. Two men worked fast to install a new front window. Though he'd had to pay double for the after-hours service, Reed didn't mind the money as much as he hated having to listen to the installers express their opinion that this entire incident was the beginning of the curse.

When the phone rang, Reed knew it couldn't be good news. It was Peter Rasinski, calling from home.

"They're talking about calling a council meeting."

"This isn't big enough for that." Reed rubbed the back of his neck. "There's no reason for the council to meet."

"What do you expect? When there's a drive-by at the police chief's house, we've got serious gang problems."

"You know very well there are no gangs in Leaning Tree." From the corner of his eye he saw Brie emerge from her room, making her way to the kitchen.

"Then who? Who would do such a thing?"

"I don't know." Oh, he suspected, but he sure as hell couldn't elaborate, even to one of his own men.

"Has to be kids. Teenagers. The entire town's up in arms about this."

"I understand why." Keeping his tone level, Reed braced himself for the question he was sure would follow.

Peter didn't disappoint him. "Boss, do you suppose this has anything to do with that woman you've got living there?"

"That woman has a name." He glanced at her, watching him from the doorway, so quiet and pale. Her haunted expression reflected his own doubts.

"Brie, then." Peter snorted. "She's living with you and you've got that, er, curse. You know?"

"Peter." Reed let his voice carry a warning. "If I hear one more thing about that damn curse, I'm going to explode. Brie and I are not in a relationship, therefore she's in no danger whatsoever from my curse. Hell hounds, you know me better than that!"

"Sorry. But I'm just asking you the same thing the council's going to ask you on Friday. People are talking. The gunshot had to be an attempt on her. They say she's gone to see the bell and—"

"Enough," Reed snarled, keeping his voice down

with difficulty. "I'll talk to you later, at the meeting." Slamming the phone down, he looked up to see Brie exiting waiflike from the room. "Wait."

She stopped, turning slowly. "I found the box. His little gift. He sent me bones from an animal. Do you have any idea what it means?"

"No."

"I need to find another place to stay."

"No." He was amazed how the thought made his gut clench. "No, you don't. Not now. Especially not now."

"I didn't want to involve you in this. The stalker's after me."

"I'm the police chief. A cop. Protect and defend, that's what I do. And I've declared myself your Nya. I'm involved whether you like it or not."

"Everyone thinks this is because of your curse. My staying here has opened up that entire can of worms again."

"I don't care." He crossed his arms to keep from touching her. "They're idiots."

Her mulish expression told him she wasn't buying it. He wanted to shake her—no, he admitted savagely, he wanted to kiss her. Wanted to resume what they'd been doing when the window had been shot out. Wisely, he kept himself still, kept his distance, his hands to himself.

"Whoever called didn't seem to think so. From what I could hear on your end, and from the neighbors earlier, this entire town seems to blame the curse."

"Would you rather they blamed you?" Despite his warnings to himself, he took a step toward her. "What difference does what they think make? We've got to catch this guy, plain and simple."

She made a sound of agreement. "You're right. And I have to tell you, all this nonsense about your supposed curse is getting on my nerves. You handle it way better than I would."

Nonsense? Supposed curse? Just like that, she erased centuries of bitter history. Not to mention his own, painful memories. He wished he could forget so easily.

She cleared her throat. He refocused, noting how her brave smile didn't match the sorrow in her eyes.

"Are you all right?"

"No, I'm not, actually. I'm beating myself up a bit here. I came here to Leaning Tree for two reasons—one, to meet my newfound family and two, to prove my mother didn't commit suicide. I've done a lot of the first, but made no progress on the last. Maybe if I'd been more proactive, none of this would have happened."

"I disagree."

"Really?" She frowned at him. "Let me know if I'm completely off base here, but I'm thinking whoever shot at me has nothing to do with the curse and everything to do with my stalker. Furthermore, I believe this is the same person who killed my mother."

Uncrossing his arms, he kept his fists clenched, just in case he got a sudden urge to touch her. "I think you're wrong. I've told you before—your stalker isn't angry at you. He doesn't believe we'll catch him and he doesn't want to kill you, just scare you. Look at the gift, for chrissakes!" He took a deep breath. "Sorry."

She stared. Blinked. "Don't be."

Running a hand through his hair, he changed the subject. "They're talking about having a special meeting of the council on Friday night. As police chief, I'd have to attend."

"Because of this?"

"Yes. I was hoping the council wouldn't get involved.

They still might not. They haven't announced an actual meeting. So far, it's all gossip."

"Is this city council?"

"Pack council. Similar, though."

At the word *Pack*, she winced. "I don't suppose you still want to help me see if I can become, a, that is…"

"Change?"

Giving a brusque nod, she watched him intently.

"Agreeing to become someone's Nya is never taken lightly. We have a date, remember? Saturday, in the woods. We're not going to let some crazy person with their own agenda ruin our plans." He held out his hand. After a moment's hesitation, she took it. As usual, touching her sent a shock through his system. He ignored it.

"Neither of us has eaten. I'm starving. How about you?"

Though she looked dubious, she nodded. "I guess I could eat something."

"Let's grill a couple of T-bones and nuke two potatoes. I always think better on a full stomach."

Later, after they'd eaten their fill—Brie even gnawing on the bone for the last pieces of meat—she brought up the council meeting again.

"If they have it, can I go? I'd really like to meet this council."

"No. You're not Pack."

At his blunt words, she looked hurt.

"I'm sorry." With a major effort, he kept himself from taking her hand. "Until you've changed, until you've proved that you can shift, they won't consider you Pack."

"Proved that I can? I thought that was a given, since I have shifter blood from my mother?"

"Rarely, and only rarely, a halfling has difficulty

changing. I doubt that's the case with you, especially since your father started you on medication. Still, until you've changed at least once, the council won't recognize you as Pack."

"But I'm going to try to change on Saturday. That's the morning after the proposed date of the meeting. What's one day?"

He shook his head. "If they have it Friday, you can't go. You can make the next one, okay? After you've changed."

"Until then, I'm still an outsider?" Without waiting for his answer, she continued. "I should be used to that by now, but you know, I don't think I'll ever get used to it."

"Used to what?"

"Being an outsider." She sighed. "I moved around a lot as a kid—I guess my dad wanted to keep one step ahead of anyone who might be looking for us. Every new school, I started out as an outsider. Most times, I didn't fit in."

He felt a pang of commiseration. "I remember you, when you lived here before. You were a cute kid. Happy, well-adjusted. Loved."

"Then my mother died and everything changed. My dad took me on the run."

"You don't know that," he protested. The look she gave him told him she wasn't going to argue the point, but she believed her own words.

"You never left?"

"Not really. Except for college, I've lived here my entire life."

Her smile looked sad. "I envy people who had that kind of permanence. Just to have the same friends—growing up with them, attending their weddings, their children's birthday parties. I'll never have that."

The hurt in her voice made him feel reckless. Even

though he'd had to deal with his own ostracism and the curse, he'd still had much of what she'd so wistfully mentioned. "You will from now on. You're here. You've got family, friends. Things are different."

"Maybe." But she didn't look convinced. "Yet once again, I'm the new person. The outsider. I'm not Pack. I'm weird. I've never changed into a wolf."

The phone rang again as he was about to speak. For half a second, Reed debated not answering it, but he was police chief. He always had to be available.

"I heard about the shooting." Malcolm's sonorous voice boomed over the line. "Is Brie all right?"

"She's fine." Reed shot her a look. "Would you like to speak with her?"

"No need. I was calling to ask you to come twenty minutes early to the meeting Friday. The council would like to talk to you privately. We'd like some answers before we speak to the townspeople."

Father Malcolm was on the council. Reed hoped having an uncle in such a position would work in his favor. Still, he could only tell the council—and the townspeople—the truth. "I don't have a whole lot of answers myself."

"You must know why someone shot your front window out." Malcolm's tone left no room for doubt.

"Not really."

"Suspicions then."

"I have a few of those. Not any I'm comfortable sharing yet."

Malcolm harrumphed. "Do the best you can then, all right?"

They concluded the call with Reed agreeing to arrive early.

Barely had he replaced the receiver when the phone rang again. "It's your aunt Marilyn." Reed handed her the phone, glad to let someone else deflect questions for once.

But Brie's conversation with her aunt was brief. She listened, nodding silently, and said nothing. Finally, she rolled her eyes and pointed at him. "Aunt Marilyn wants to talk to me before the big meeting as well," Brie said, handing him the phone. "But right now, she wants to talk to you."

After reassuring Marilyn—and through her, the entire Beswick clan—that he'd protect Brie, Reed ended the call.

"Sorry." Brie shrugged. "I don't know why she thinks we're holding out on her."

"I don't know, but my uncle Malcolm said much the same thing to me. The council wants to talk to me before the big meeting on Friday. Makes me feel like a teenager again, in trouble for some petty misdeed."

"Oh?" She raised a brow. "Were you in trouble often?"

"Often enough that I went home a few times with my tail between my legs." His use of a canine analogy didn't even startle her. She grinned instead.

"We ought to get some sleep."

Her grin faded. Her quick, uncertain glance at the new window made him want to pull her close and comfort her. "That's a good idea, I think."

"No one's going to bother us again tonight. I think whoever it was has had his fun for the day." Keeping his distance, Reed used the same tone he'd use for soothing a lost child.

Though she nodded, her expression still appeared haunted. As she walked off to go to her room, she turned and looked at him. "Reed, tomorrow I'd like to be more hands-on. The stalker has stepped things up a notch. I need to do the same."

Chapter 12

Thursday dawned with a brilliant sunrise. Not a cloud marred the perfect sky. Since she'd been unable to sleep, Brie had risen at five and padded out to the kitchen to make a pot of coffee. Cup in hand, she'd stepped out on the back porch, into the warm darkness, to watch the pink tendrils blossom on the horizon as the sky lightened.

She worried about this change she was supposed to do on Saturday. Would the earth move in two days? She blushed, glad Reed still slept. Though she'd stopped taking her allergy pills three days ago, she'd expected to feel different. More wild, uninhibited, somehow. And, being skeptical, she'd definitely thought the sinus problems her father had so often warned her of would manifest themselves. But she hadn't so much as sneezed. No watery eyes, nothing.

It would appear Reed and everyone else had been

right. Her father must have lied about the allergy medications. Knowing that made her question everything
else he'd ever told her. She'd loved her father, looked
up to him, and now the safety net of her upbringing had
been shredded. Here she was, in Leaning Tree, N.Y.,
about to take a flying leap into the cavernous unknown.

Grinning at her poetic nature this morning, Brie
drained the last of her mug and went inside to get more
coffee. As her eyes adjusted to the shadowy interior, she
made out a familiar shape lounging against the door frame.

Reed. Her heart leaped in her chest. "Good morning."

"Is it?" He ran a hand through sleep-tousled hair.
Shirtless, he wore a pair of faded cotton shorts that rode
low on his waist. With his morning stubble and muscular chest, the sight of him made her ache.

She was only human. When presented with such
temptation, how did he think she'd react?

She turned away, busying herself with adding
creamer and sugar to her drink. "I couldn't sleep."

"Worried? Or excited?"

If he only knew. Somehow sex and Reed had gotten
tangled up in her concept of this…changing. Maybe
because her feelings for Reed were constantly shifting,
undergoing their own sort of change.

Geez, she was positively philosophical this morning.
Bad poetry and philosophy, coffee instead of gin. "I've
been thinking a lot about Saturday."

He moved closer, and her heartbeat tripled. "Eager,
huh?"

She felt utterly foolish when he sidled past her, heading for the coffeepot and his own morning jolt.

Still, the scent of him tickled her nose. He smelled
like man and sleep and something else, something in-

definable. Musk? Mint? A combination of the two, she decided. Her sense of smell, at least where Reed was concerned, seemed to have grown at the same pace as her attraction.

"I guess. Only two more days. I was wondering if I needed to do anything in advance to prepare."

"No, not really. Saturday, just don't wear a lot of clothes. Most women wear a sundress or something. Easy on, easy off."

Perplexed, she frowned. "What do you mean?"

"You have to take your clothes off before you change." He smiled. She could swear he was enjoying her discomfort.

"Naked? You…I…we…?"

"You can't change with your clothes on. They'll tear."

She hadn't thought of that. Great. When—if—she and Reed ever got naked together, she would have preferred different circumstances.

"Oh. No big deal, then." She went for feigned nonchalance, though her cheeks were burning. Change the subject. "What's on your agenda for today?"

"After I check in at the station, I thought I'd look up some of your mother's old friends, talk to them. Though it's been a long time, you never know if they might remember something."

"I want to go."

He nodded his head. "Of course you do. You said you wanted to be proactive. You can come along."

"Great." Embarrassment forgotten, she set her mug down on the counter. "When do you want to leave? I'll need a few minutes to get ready."

"A few minutes?" His grin was wicked and sensual. "I've never known a woman who could do that."

Transfixed, she stared, then, giving herself a mental shake, grinned back. "Okay, maybe I was a bit hasty. Half an hour? I need to shower and—" looking him up and down in an exaggerated leer, she sniffed "—so do you."

Head held high, she exited the kitchen to the warm sound of his masculine laughter.

An hour later, Reed signaled a right turn. "I've made a list of people your mother knew, using those old case files. We're almost to Robert McCutchen's place. He was her boyfriend all through high school. They were pretty serious, though they split up when she started dating Scott Wells."

Her mother's other old beau was a portly man with a shock of silver-streaked hair and a goatee. Happily married, he reminisced about his old girlfriend with his arm around his wife Carol's shoulders.

Brie exchanged a glance with Reed. While she enjoyed hearing stories about her mother's high school days, this wasn't what she was looking for. Finally, Reed stood and, claiming another appointment, they took their leave.

"Nice guy," she commented as she climbed into the pickup.

"Yeah, but you're not going to like who's next." He handed her his list. "Top of the second page. Take a look."

"Eldon Brashear? He was one of my mother's friends?" Brie couldn't keep the skepticism from her voice. "I find that hard to imagine."

"He wasn't exactly a friend. She dumped him." Reed drove confidently, the same way he did everything. But even spoken in his self-assured tone, his words gave Brie pause.

For the first time since they'd come up with this plan, Brie felt a premonition, a chill of warning. "Reed, while we're there, can we try to find out why Eldon Brashear hates me so much? I mean, he literally despises me— and we've only met the one time when I accidentally trespassed on his land. Oh, and when he rear-ended me."

"Evidently Eldon holds a grudge a long time."

"A grudge? I've never done anything to the man."

"No, but you look just like your mother, Brie. And, real or imaginary, I think Eldon never got over her breaking up with him."

"When was this? You said she dated Robert McCutchen and Scott Wells. Where did Eldon fit in?"

"When she got back from college, she hooked up with Eldon. Then she met your dad, and that was it."

Brie stared. "Great. Why didn't you mention this earlier?"

"Eldon's always seemed harmless. I decided to wait and see if I could gather more evidence."

"Harmless? The guy's a raving psycho!"

"Hold on, Brie." Reed lifted his hand, his expression serious. "Don't jump to conclusions. We don't know for sure it's him. We have no proof. He's an old man. Hell, he was middle-aged twenty-five years ago, when he asked your mother out. That's why no one could understand why someone as young and beautiful as Elizabeth would date him."

"Me either."

"And he's too obvious to be the stalker. I'd think if he was, he'd keep a low profile. But we're going to check him out anyway, just to make sure."

She slid lower in her seat. "How's he going to react when he sees me with you?"

"Maybe you should wait in the truck."

"Wait in the truck?" She raised herself to her full height. "No way. I want to talk to him. I want to be there if he says something that gives him away."

Familiar with the grouchy old man, Reed phoned ahead to let Eldon know they were coming. Though Eldon demanded to know why, Reed informed him they'd discuss it in person when he arrived.

"You didn't mention me," Brie said, when he clicked his cell phone closed. "Don't you think you should've warned him I was with you?"

"Nah." Reed grinned at her. "Don't want to raise his blood pressure in advance."

"Maybe surprise will work to our advantage and he'll slip up."

"Don't assume guilt without justifiable cause. Just because he seems a likely suspect doesn't mean he's the perpetrator."

Brie studied him. He felt her gaze like a touch. "Cop face, cop uniform, cop voice and cop words. Yep, you must be in law enforcement."

He laughed, feeling the tension ease slightly. "But seriously, you don't know how many times we have a suspect we *know* did the crime. But there's no proof, or not enough proof and we have no choice but to let the guy go." He turned down a long, dirt road. "Here we are."

"Wow!" Brie said when she saw the house. Eldon Brashear's place looked surprisingly well kept. "I expected a run-down, junked-out, unpainted shack." Instead, Eldon lived in a tidy, white frame ranch house. Freshly painted, the place looked as welcoming as the man was not. Parked in front of an equally neat garage, his beat-up, old pickup truck appeared distinctly out of place.

Reed grinned again at her stunned reaction. "Come on." He touched her arm, searching her face for signs of nervousness. "Eldon's waiting."

"I know, but he gives me the creeps." She swallowed hard. "I keep thinking about the hatred I see in his eyes every time he looks at me."

Reed wanted to put his hand on her shoulder, a gesture of comfort, but knew touching her again would be a mistake. "You'll be fine," he said, instead.

"I know." Lifting her chin, she got out of the truck. Despite her brave words, she stayed close to him, standing slightly behind him when he rang the doorbell.

The door swung open soundlessly.

"Come on in." Eldon's gaze narrowed when he saw Brie. He spat a wad of chewing tobacco into a plant near the doorstep, narrowly missing her foot. "You!" He rounded on Reed. "You didn't say nothin' about her. What'd you bring her for?"

Reed shepherded Brie inside. "We've got a few questions for you."

Still holding the door wide open, Eldon's mouth worked. "Since when does the Leaning Tree police force solicit the help of bimbos?"

Brie stiffened. "Listen here, you old—"

"She's not a bimbo." Reed kept his tone soothing, standing between the old man and Brie. "She wants to ask you about her mother."

"Her mother!" Eldon spewed invectives—and spittle. Stepping back, and wiping his face with the back of his hand, Reed motioned the older man toward the couch. "Close the door and take a seat, why don't you."

"Am I under arrest?" With a scowl, Eldon stayed put.

Reed regarded him steadily. "Have you done something you need to be arrested for, Eldon?"

Eldon's gaze darted to Brie. "If this is about that traffic accident, get with my insurance company. They've already told her they'd pay to fix her damn car."

"This is not about the accident. I told you, we want to ask you about Elizabeth Beswick."

At the name, Eldon's lined face creased into a bitter mask. "I don't want to talk about her. If you ain't arresting me, you need to leave."

"But—" Brie stepped forward.

Eldon snarled, baring his teeth as though he thought he was a wolf.

Reed sensed if he was pushed too much further, the older man might change right there in front of them, while still enraged. A furious wolf was deadly, uncontrollable.

"We're going." Reed took Brie's arm and moved her toward the still open door. "Don't argue," he told her, *sotto voce*. "Just go."

The instant they stepped outside, Eldon slammed the door shut.

"He's a fool." Reed helped a shaken Brie into the truck before going around to his side and climbing in. "Stone cold fool."

"A fool? How about a stalker? A murderer? He's crazy. It's entirely possible he did it," Brie said flatly after he'd started the engine. "And yes, I'm aware I don't have proof. But I'd bet my last dollar he's the one."

"I'm not so sure. It's hard to tell if he's just a crotchety old cuss, or a bitter, dangerous man bent on revenge for imagined insults over twenty years ago. He's been living alone his entire life, ever since his mother died when he was thirty."

She sighed. "Who's next?"

"We're heading to the west side of town to talk to several ladies. They were your mama's best friends. They're still close, and they all live within a few miles of each other."

Three hours later they broke for lunch. Sliding into a booth at Smokey Joe's, they ordered sliced beef sandwiches with potato salad and iced tea.

"Though I'm more certain than ever Eldon's the one, we haven't learned anything new." Brie's despair leaked into her voice.

"No, but one rarely does at first." Reed was optimistic. "We've learned a lot about your mother's life, and we've established a routine. We'll finish interviewing the others this afternoon and see if anything turns up."

She sat back in the booth, gaze steady. "Then what?"

"We step back, look at the big picture. Then we find the one anomaly, the thing that rips the picture apart."

By suppertime they'd talked to every name on the list save one. Father Malcolm. Just hearing the name appeared to make Brie relax. "I'm glad you saved him for last. He's a nice way to end a long day."

Reed smiled. "Let me give him a call and make sure he's got time to see us." He punched in the number at the church from memory. His uncle answered on the third ring, surprised, but willing to meet with them in fifteen minutes.

As usual, the instant they walked into the sanctuary, Reed felt his tension leave him. He loved this church, and though he'd rarely attended mass since Teresa died, the beauty of the sanctuary brought him a sense of comfort.

Dressed in his black cassock, Malcolm hurried out to greet them. After kissing Brie on the cheek, he clapped Reed on the back.

"How are you two?" Malcolm asked fondly.

"Tired." Again Reed caught himself about to slip his arm around Brie's shoulders. Shaking his head, he glanced at his uncle and forced a smile. "It's been a long day."

"I understand. Come on back to my kitchen. We can talk there. I'd offer you coffee, but there's none made. It's too late in the day and I can't sleep if I drink caffeine after five." He strolled off ahead of them, disappearing behind his sliding doors.

Brie smiled up at Reed, her eyes glowing. Reed felt the beauty of that smile like a punch to the gut. Then, while he was still recovering, she slipped her arm in his and leaned close. Her peach scent made him momentarily dizzy.

"I bet if you ask him, your uncle will think Eldon Brashear is our stalker," she whispered.

Reed shook his head, extracting himself so he could think. "Later. I don't want him—or anyone else—taking sides. The last thing we need in Leaning Tree is a vendetta against an innocent man. We've got to gather proof. We have to be sure, beyond a reasonable doubt."

Once they'd all taken seats at the table, Reed recounted how they'd spent their day. When he finished, his uncle clucked thoughtfully.

"I agree with Brie that Eldon Brashear is an excellent suspect." The priest's direct gaze swept over Reed. "And I agree with you that you must have better proof. We cannot bring this up before the council without more evidence."

"I know."

"But I have one more name for you to consider. What about Scott Wells?"

Reed frowned. "We've talked to him. He seems harmless."

"Though he did shoot out my back window," Brie said. "He thought I was a trespasser."

"See what I mean?" Malcolm looked at Reed. "Scott obsessed over Elizabeth—she told me so. She was frightened of him, especially when he wouldn't leave her alone. How do you know he's not stalking Brie?"

"We don't. We're checking out all angles."

Malcolm turned his attention to Brie. "You shouldn't be alone."

She smiled at his blunt words. "I'm not. I'm staying with Reed, remember?"

"Yes, but he has to work." Including Reed in his gaze, he leaned forward. "He can't be with you every second of every day."

"She has her family," Reed put in. "You know how many Beswicks there are. When she's not with me, she's with them."

"Are you?" With a kind smile, Father Malcolm shook his head. "Then how is it possible that every time I see you, you're by yourself?"

Her eyes widened. "Usually I'm coming from my aunt's house to Reed's, or here to the church. I'm safe in my car, aren't I?"

Though she'd asked Reed, the priest answered. "What if your stalker decides to run into you, or run you off the road? If memory serves me correctly, Eldon Brashear has a large truck."

"Had a large truck," Reed put in dryly. "He rear-ended Brie and wrecked it. I'm not sure the thing is drivable now."

"Oh, it must be. I saw Eldon in town yesterday afternoon."

"Great." Brie shook her head. "That's all I need."

Reed glanced at his watch and stood. "We've taken up enough of your time. We'll get going and let you have your dinner, Uncle Malcolm."

Brie got to her feet. "Thank you so much." She hugged the older man. He hugged her back, then, holding her at arm's length, he studied her.

"Have you changed yet?"

Brie looked at Reed before turning back to Malcolm. "Not yet. We have plans to try on Saturday."

"We?"

"Reed and I."

"Ah, I see." Malcolm released her, pinching the bridge of his nose. "So Reed will be your Nya?"

"Yes." Reed took Brie's arm. "We've really got to go."

"Wait." Tone urgent, Malcolm stepped forward. "It may not be a good idea for you to be her Nya."

"Of course it is," Brie interceded. "I can't think of anyone I trust more. And my mother was his Nya, way back when."

This seemed to surprise the older man. "She was? I didn't know that."

"You were in seminary." Restless, Reed steered Brie toward the door. "I was only seven."

The priest chuckled wryly. "I remember you then. Your brother used to send me pictures." He was still smiling as they walked out the door.

"I'd like to learn more about my mother." Brie sighed. "Sometimes I get so caught up in trying to solve her death that I forget to try to learn about what kind of person she was."

"She was warm and giving. Everyone loved her," Reed said.

"Even you?"

"Yes." He grinned. "I had the worst crush on her. I might have been only seven when she became my Nya, but even I knew a hottie when I met one."

"Hey!" Brie swatted him. "That's my mother you're talking about."

"Seriously." Reed shook his head. "Elizabeth Beswick was beautiful. Both in body and in spirit. She adored your father, loved him enough to marry outside the Pack. He worshipped her, so much so he was willing to uproot his life and move here so their children could be raised among their own kind."

"Their own kind." Expression thoughtful, Brie climbed into the truck. She waited until Reed was buckled in, then asked, "Is marrying outside the Pack uncommon?"

"Back then it was." He grinned. "These days a lot of our young men look for their mates in other places. Some travel to other packs, others work in mostly human cities. Both Alex Lupe and his sister Brenna married human mates."

"Mates…" she mused. "Seems an odd choice of words."

Mates. The word made him long to touch her. As if he had any right. He struggled to focus. "Not really. Like the wolves we become, we mate for life."

Brie thought of Reed's wife, Teresa, and wondered what happened when a Pack male lost his mate. Were they able to find another? "Is it such a hard thing, to find someone with whom you're compatible?"

He laughed. "It's more than that, Brie. When one of the Pack meets his true mate, he knows."

The way Reed knew Brie could be his, if he weren't living under that damn curse.

The expression on his handsome face, as if holding some raw emotion in check, tugged at Brie deep inside. To distract herself, she focused on his last statement.

"How? How would one know they'd met their mate?" Once she'd asked the question, she found she really wanted to know. The complex feelings Reed aroused in her overwhelmed her and made her wonder about his place in her life, curse or no curse.

With an apparent effort at nonchalance, he shrugged. "I don't know—maybe one can't imagine life without the other. Maybe one's willing to risk everything to be with the other."

Risk everything. She shivered. "Sounds like love to me."

"Love revved up another notch," he agreed. "You'll have to meet Alex and his wife Lyssa or Brenna and Carson. When you see them together, you'll know what I mean."

Again she wondered about Reed's wife Teresa, then immediately chastised herself. Why would she want to know anyway? Did she plan on interviewing for the position?

"That's interesting. Is there somewhere I can learn more about shifters and the Pack? You mentioned the church has a collection of books. Do you think your uncle would let me look at them?"

"Probably. Your best bet is your aunt Marilyn. She has a massive, private collection. She inherited a ton of books from her own aunt. I get the impression they're passed down from generation to generation."

"So her daughter Edie will get them next?"

"Maybe so. Next Beswick female, I think. That might even be you. I'm not sure what criteria they use. Your aunt could probably tell you."

Brie made a mental note to ask. She'd check out the books at the church as well. Whether or not this shape-shifter stuff was real, she'd love to know how long such a belief had existed, and learn the history of her adopted new town. And, somewhere in all of this, she might find something relating to her mother's death.

"I'm meeting my aunt for lunch tomorrow. Friday's are her day off from volunteer work. I'll ask her then."

The next morning, sitting in Reed's cozy kitchen after he'd left for work, Brie read over the old case files once more. She kept thinking she might find something she'd missed. But nothing new leaped out at her.

She didn't know where to go from here. While she had her suspicions about Eldon Brashear, she couldn't confront the man. Not yet. Not without more evidence. More and more, it looked as though she might need to work out a plan to flush out the stalker, lure him into meeting her. If she could get Reed to agree, which she doubted. There was no way she wanted to try and handle such an undertaking alone.

Finally, it was time to meet her aunt. Brie had suggested they meet at one of the downtown restaurants but Aunt Marilyn had pooh-poohed the idea.

"I cook so much better than any of them," she'd boasted with a wink. "Come by and I'll make my famous chicken salad."

Arriving shortly after noon, Brie started to press the doorbell, then, remembering her aunt's instructions, dug in her purse for the key she'd been told to keep. She let herself in, feeling a pang of homesickness, marveling at the way the place always smelled so…deliciously homey.

"I can't believe I can actually smell the apples." Walking into the kitchen, Brie kissed her aunt on the cheek. Marilyn grinned, waving her over to the kitchen table, where two glasses of iced tea and lemon waited. "I grilled the chicken earlier, so it'd be nice and fresh when I cut it up."

Brie took a sip from her drink and watched while the older woman bustled happily around the bright kitchen. She brought over two salad plates brimming with the apples and grapes, lettuce, tomatoes and thinly sliced grilled chicken. She drizzled balsamic vinaigrette dressing over the top. Just looking at it made Brie's mouth water.

"Dig in." Aunt Marilyn dropped into a chair and picked up her fork.

Spearing a piece of chicken, Brie popped it in her mouth. When she'd finished chewing, she rolled her eyes skyward. "You weren't kidding. This is wonderful!"

Neither spoke again until the food was gone.

"Divine." Placing her fork on the cleaned plate, Brie shook her head. "I've never tasted a salad—any salad— like that. You've got a rare talent, Aunt Marilyn."

"Thank you." The older woman carried the dishes to the sink, waving away Brie's offer to wash them. "I'll do them later. Right now I want to show you those letters we talked about. I've kept them, all these years. We need to talk about your stalker."

Chapter 13

Brie waited impatiently for Reed to return home from work. Not only was tomorrow *the* day, but seeing her aunt's letters had unsettled her, and she needed to discuss what she'd learned with law enforcement. Pacing, she snorted. Law enforcement, indeed. Who was she kidding? Herself? She needed Reed. No one else.

Finally, headlights swept the bay window. Listening to the sound of the garage door opening, she stopped her pacing long enough to wait, heart pounding, in the kitchen so he'd see her the second he came through the door.

"Brie?" He crossed the room quickly, stopping a few feet from her. "What is it? Is everything all right?"

She couldn't stop twisting her hands together, a habit she'd thought she'd abolished in adolescence. "I saw Aunt Marilyn's letters, the ones she got from the stalker. There's no doubt about it now. They were the same."

Reed narrowed his eyes. "What do you mean?"

"Exactly that. Typed on an old typewriter, faint letter *e*, all of it. The wording, language, everything. This stalker is targeting Beswick women, and has been for years."

"And now you." Glancing at the clock, Reed swore. "It's too late for us to run over there. I'd like to take a look at them. When did she start getting them?"

"A few months before she married Uncle Albert." Brie took a deep breath. "She wasn't aware that my mother had gotten them."

"Elizabeth didn't confide in anyone. None of her friends or family knew anything about a stalker." He jabbed his finger in the direction of the table, where the case folders were still stacked. "Nothing was mentioned in the report either, so we know she didn't go to the police. What I don't understand is why didn't Marilyn report it?"

"I saw them, read through them. They're more like the early ones my mother got—as if the writer is courting her. Nothing threatening, no reason to be alarmed. She showed them to Uncle Albert, and he wasn't concerned either. So she put them away and hasn't thought about them for years. Until she'd learned I'd gotten one."

"What about your cousins? They're the only other Beswick females, besides you. Have they received any letters?"

"I haven't discussed any of this with them. I had no reason to. I doubt Aunt Marilyn's mentioned it either."

"We need to talk to them."

"I will, though I think they'd have told their mother." She took a deep breath. "Reed, there's more. Aunt Marilyn thinks Scott Wells is the one who's stalking me."

He froze. "Does she have any proof?"

"No. But she says he dated her, too, before she married Uncle Albert. And after my mom married my dad, Scott overdosed on drugs."

Reed nodded. "But has he done anything recently to make her think he's started up again?"

"I don't think so. She didn't say."

She looked up and caught Reed staring at her with a look of such tenderness on his face it took her breath away. "Reed?"

He shook his head and his expression once again became the remote, professional face of a cop. "We'll call your aunt tomorrow afternoon, so I can go look at the letters." He walked to the kitchen door, looking over his shoulder at her. Shadows hid his expression. "Try and get some sleep. Tomorrow's Saturday. A big day for you."

As if she didn't know. From somewhere deep inside her, she pulled forth a shaky smile. She really wanted to cross the room, pull his face down to hers and kiss the hell out of him. "Good night, Reed."

"'Night." The sound of his door closing seemed to echo down the hall.

Brie went to her own room, though she doubted she'd sleep. Her nerves were jangling. She had a strong sense she was missing something, some little detail, that tied everything together. Whatever it was, it continued to elude her.

She lay down on her bed, fully dressed, and watched the soft green glow of the numerals on her alarm clock until her eyes drifted closed, wondering how foolish she would feel when she went into the woods with Reed in the morning.

When she woke at 6:52 a.m., the sun had risen. Fi-

nally, Saturday morning. The big day. Despite her skepticism, part of her really hoped… She shook her head.
No matter what happened, her entire body thrummed
with excitement. She couldn't help herself. Though
technically she knew there were no such things as werewolves, the entire towns' belief had made her think of
the possibility.

Right. She chided herself. How had she gone from a
rational skeptic to a goofily optimistic, misguided fa-
natic standing in a field waiting for a UFO to show up
and beam her on board?

Hurrying through her morning preparations, she
showered, got dressed and headed down to the kitchen,
heart pounding so hard it felt like it would burst from
her chest. Reed waited out on the back porch, staring
into the woods. Early morning sun shone through the
tall trees, dappling the leaves with vibrant gold. Wrens
and sparrows flew and chirped, welcoming the new day,
which promised to be warm. A crow cawed, another responded. A soft rustle in the underbrush spoke of a rabbit's quiet passage.

Brie registered none of these things. She focused all
of her attention on the man who stood next to her.
Though she tried to appear calm, she felt far from it. Her
palms were clammy, her entire body trembled. Even her
breathing sounded ragged, as though she'd gone for an
early morning run.

All because there was the most remote possibility she
could somehow change into a werewolf.

She should feel silly, not scared. Humiliated rather
than hopeful. In a moment she would have to strip naked, in front of the one man she wanted more than any
other. And then what?

"Are you ready?" Low-voiced, Reed stood a few feet from her. At her nod, he led the way across his lawn. At the edge of the forest, he kicked off his flip-flops and shimmied his jean shorts down, stepping out of them.

Wide-eyed, Brie couldn't keep from staring. He wore nothing underneath. Talk about beauty—au naturel, Reed Hunter looked like a classical statue. An extremely well-endowed statue. Her entire body heated.

Practically panting, she averted her gaze.

"Your turn." She could hear the grin in his voice. She took a deep breath. She could do this, she could. She shivered again, her nipples hard from the early morning chill and her irrational excitement. Still without looking at him, Brie lifted her sundress over her head and let it fall to the ground at her feet.

Naked, she stood next to the man her entire body craved, preparing for something straight out of a horror novel.

She heard the harsh intake of his breath as he viewed her naked for the first time. She refused to look at him, embarrassed and aroused, feeling foolish and exhilarated, all at once.

"Are you ready?" he asked again.

She nodded, heart in her throat.

"Good. Now, I want you to listen. Listen like you've never listened before, with more than your ear. With your heart, your soul. If you try, you can hear the pulse of the earth's heart beating. The sounds of morning, of the forest are all around you."

She did as he asked, hearing the rustles small creatures made and birdsong—the cry of the crow, the warbling of the robin.

"Now *feel*. The air on your skin. The resonance of

the earth's pulse beneath your feet. Inhale. Breathe. And smell. Use your nose as nature meant you to. Draw in the warm richness of the forest."

Again she complied. This time, something shifted inside her. A small movement, like her bones were re-aligning.

The feeling startled her. Her gaze flew to Reed, who smiled reassuringly.

"Think of yourself as a wolf. Picture your fur, your muzzle, paws, your teeth."

Though she tried, she couldn't imagine such a thing. She kept seeing Michael J. Fox in that old movie, *Teen Wolf.* If not for her nervousness, she'd giggle.

She looked down at herself and saw human legs, human feet. Touched her arm and felt human skin.

"Look at me." Reed's softly spoken command had her instinctively turning her head. She didn't know what she expected, but one look at his fully aroused body and she swayed. Looked again, and blinked. Shimmers of moving color and flicks of bright light danced around him, like a swarm of joyful fireflies.

"Reed?"

"I'm changing," he said, and even his voice was lower, more guttural.

As she watched, the swirling collage of sparks obscured him from view.

When the light pulses faded, a huge, black wolf stood where Reed had been.

No way! She staggered back, gasping. Despite all she'd been told, this wasn't possible. Man to wolf, human to beast. It couldn't be real.

Then, while she gaped, her own body responded. Knees buckling, she dropped to the ground, on all fours.

The edges of her vision grayed, and she shook her head as a moan escaped her.

Again she saw the flashing lights, though this time they swirled around her.

Now. Here. Human. Bones. Blood.

Something pulled at her, she felt her body lengthen, her very cells transmuting into something else, something not quite human, though still fully female. She was still Brie, Brie, Brie, Brie...

Now wolf.

She lifted her muzzle and let out a howl.

Confusion and exhilaration warred inside her. They'd been telling the truth, each and every one of them. She was a shifter, Pack. Finally, she belonged.

Reed padded over to her and touched her nose with his. His scent enveloped her—male and musk and wolf. Wolf, not man.

Amazed, she inspected herself, wondering what color wolf she'd become. In the grayscale of her new vision, her coat appeared to be pearly silver, so pale she looked nearly white.

A glow-in-the-dark wolf. She bared her teeth in a grin.

Grinning back, tongue lolling, Reed took off running, making circles around her, the flash of his black coat a tantalizing lure. Then he disappeared into the shadowy forest, moving hard and fast and silent.

Gone. She was alone. Wolf.

Cautiously she stretched, and then took off after him. Clumsily at first, not sure how to move. Her paws connected to the earth, and her stride lengthened as she became accustomed to her new body. As wolf, she felt like a bundle of power, all nerves and sinew and bones.

An hour or more later—she had no way to calculate the passing of time—she returned to the glade where she'd left her dress, exhausted and weak.

She lay on her belly, relishing the feel of the cool, damp earth, and panted, trying to think.

The only world she'd ever known, the human world, seemed very far away.

How did she change back? As soon as she wondered, she knew. She thought of herself as human and the curious tingling began again. Her bones shifted, compressed. Her heart rate slowed. Closing her eyes to block out the bright flashes of light, she felt her body rearrange itself. Finally, she wore skin instead of fur.

She was woman once more. Human. Shocked and exhilarated. With adrenaline still surging through her, she stepped to her discarded dress and started to pull it on. She stopped when movement at the edge of the trees caught her eye. A blur of shifting light, coming toward her. A wolf. No, a man. Reed. Human. Naked.

And fully aroused.

Something tightened, low in her belly. Her pulse leaped. A shudder of raw need shook her. She'd always wanted him, she knew that. From just about the first moment she'd set eyes on him, she'd craved the feel of his hands on her skin, his mouth on hers.

He was, no matter what anyone might say, her mate.

As wolf, she'd known. As human, she could no longer deny the truth.

He stopped, his eyes dark and full of desire. She let her gaze roam over him, knowing he felt the look like a caress, thrilling to the way his breathing quickened.

Her mate. Not just her Nya. They'd changed together,

become another species and run side by side through the forest.

She took a step toward him. The very air between them seemed electrified, arcing with sparks.

She took another step. Every ounce of her body throbbed. Her blood surged. In the aftermath of her first change, feverish passion made her bold. Curse be damned.

Aching, wanting, she went to him. In her human form, the slender body she'd always taken for granted, she knew herself to be sleek, soft, supple. Senses still amplified, she inhaled his scent. Her naked skin felt like silk as she rubbed against his hard, muscular body.

He made a sound, a cross between a moan and a growl.

Desire blasted through her. He stood, all corded sinew and muscle as she stroked and rubbed and touched and caressed, nibbling and kissing and biting him.

When she reached his mouth, he took over, and slanted his lips across hers. They kissed, hard and wild and abandoned, and each time he plunged his tongue into her mouth, she shuddered, before replying in kind.

Locked together, his arousal surged against her. Mindless with passion, she pressed against him, wanting more, craving him, needing him buried inside her.

"No," he gasped, pushing away. He turned his back to her, his breathing harsh and ragged, the picture of a man in torment. Panting, he bowed his head and clenched his fists. "We can't. The curse…" He ground out the words. "I won't…"

Reality hit her with the slap of the chilly night air. He was right. And oh, so wrong. Shaking her head to clear her thoughts, Brie snatched up her dress and stepped into it. The fabric scratched against her over-sensitive skin as she pulled it up.

Then, her throat aching with unshed tears, her chest tight with a wound too deep for words, she left Reed alone. With his damn curse and the tattered remnants of her pride.

Back at the house, Brie changed to jeans and a tank top, washed her face, and headed over to her aunt Marilyn's house. Reed had not yet reappeared, which was fine with her. She didn't know how she'd face him after his rejection. Even if he'd had good reason, at least in his mind, that knowledge didn't make it any easier to bear.

Marilyn was cooking again. This time, she'd made beef brisket, and had it slow-cooking on the grill.

She welcomed Brie with open arms.

"Honey, what's wrong? You look...haunted."

Wishing she was less transparent, Brie mustered up a smile. She wasn't up to discussing her first change, not yet. She felt too...unsettled. Raw. "Just feeling a little rushed, that's all. Aunt Marilyn, I've been hearing about your library and I wondered if I could use it."

"Of course. It's the Beswick family library, after all. There are so many books, it's impossible to get through them all. Believe me, I've been trying. I've been in there a lot lately, trying to gain information about the Hunter's curse."

Brie's gaze flew to hers. "Lately it seems like everyone else is one step ahead of me. That's not a good feeling."

Her aunt laughed. "Honey, whatever is between the two of you is so sharp, the air positively sizzles. I've been trying to discover a way for the curse to be broken. You can look, too, as well as learn more about the Pack. Come with me."

Leading the way down the hall, they came to a door

which had always been closed while Brie had lived there. Pulling a huge, antique key from her pocket, Marilyn unlocked the door and led Brie inside.

"Here we are."

"You weren't kidding." Gazing around Marilyn's oak-paneled library in disbelief, Brie turned a slow circle. "There must be close to a thousand books in here."

"Maybe more," Aunt Marilyn beamed. "I haven't even been able to read them all. Some of the older ones are hard to get through." She pointed. "I use the ones in that smaller bookcase for my weekly class. I teach children how to prepare for their first change. There's lots of Pack history and such. Maybe you'd want to start with those."

Brie still didn't want to tell her aunt she'd already changed. Her emotions were too raw. Instead, she smiled and nodded. "Thanks. That makes it less daunting."

"Oh honey, you can't know how pleased I am that you're taking an interest in your heritage." Marilyn hugged her. "Your mother would be so proud."

Brie searched her aunt's face. "You know, this is the first time I've heard you mention her without sadness in your voice."

"I loved my sister." Releasing her, Marilyn smiled. "And having you here brings her back to life for me. Now I've got a potato salad to make." She left Brie alone to read.

Several hours later, after accepting her aunt's offer of a sandwich for lunch and chowing it down, Brie was still reading when Aunt Marilyn interrupted her again. "Father Malcolm is here to see you," she whispered, a frown creasing her plump face. "He says it's urgent. He claims he was driving by and saw your car."

Closing her book, Brie looked longingly at the small pile of books stacked next to her. Shaking her head, she stretched and yawned. "He's probably wanting to check on me, make sure I'm safe. He's been a bit paranoid since the shooting."

Marilyn's frown deepened. "I barely talk to the man, ever since he denied Elizabeth the right to be buried in our family plot. I don't think—"

"Brie." Father Malcolm strode into the room. Instead of his clerical garb, he wore a plaid sports jacket and slacks. "How are you?"

Glancing between her aunt and the priest, Brie held out her hand for him to shake. Ignoring this, he gathered her up in a hug, squeezing her tight. Once he'd released her, he stepped back and glanced around the room. "I must say, Marilyn, your historical collection rivals that of the church. I wasn't aware you kept such an archive."

"The Beswicks have always been historians, you know that." Marilyn's smile was stiffly polite. "I thought I asked you to wait in the parlor?"

"Did you?" Strolling around the room, he appeared supremely unconcerned. "I heard Brie's voice and thought I'd come on back. You don't mind, do you?"

"Actually, I—"

"Good, good." He plucked a book from the shelf. "I have this one at the church. It's quite good, if a bit outdated." He flipped through the pages, gave a satisfied nod, and added the book to Brie's stack. "Recommended reading, my dear."

"Okay." Brie glanced once more from Malcolm to her aunt. "Aunt Marilyn said this visit was urgent. What did you want to see me about, Father?"

His smile vanished. "I need to talk to you." He shot Marilyn a dismissive glance. "Alone."

"I—"

"It's private," he said, his voice firm but gentle.

"Fine." Marilyn threw up her hands. "I'll be in the kitchen if you need me." She stomped off, her footsteps loud as she went down the hall.

"You said this was important."

"It is."

She waited.

"Remember when you told me Reed had agreed to be your Nya, and I said it was a bad idea?"

"Yes. Is there a problem?"

"There is, there is." With a long, mournful sigh, he shook his head. "If Reed acts as your Nya when you change, you're in danger, Brie. Grave danger. I wasn't aware your mother had been his Nya. Knowing that now, proves what I've always suspected. If Reed is your Nya, you'll bring down our family curse on you."

The curse. She sighed. "Reed and I are not involved. We have no relationship. So no, the curse isn't after me."

"You're wrong. By Reed becoming your Nya, you two will have established a relationship. A close one." Expression compassionate, he squeezed her hand. "I'm sorry to tell you this, Brie. But I believe you and Reed will inadvertently bring the Hunter curse down on you if you go through with it."

She didn't have the nerve to tell him it was a done deal. If Reed acting as her Nya made her cursed, then it had already happened, that very morning.

Her first reaction was disbelief. Her second thought, one that she certainly couldn't share with the priest, was if she was already cursed, then she and Reed could finally give in to the explosive passion between them.

Had she lost her mind? If werewolves—or shifters—could exist in the world, who was she to say a curse couldn't? She should be afraid. Very afraid.

But staring at Father Malcolm, she felt only relief and eagerness. Tentative joy. But no fear. Was she so foolish to think she was invulnerable?

Malcolm watched her closely. "Are you all right?"

Startled, she realized he still held her hand. Gently, she eased her fingers free. "I need some time alone."

He nodded. "I understand.

She waited for him to leave. He made no move to do so. She took a deep breath. "Have you spoken to Reed yet?"

"I left a message for him at the office and on his cell phone. He hasn't called me back yet. When he does, I'll tell him." He shook his head sadly. "Think of yourself Brie, for once. You're the one in danger, not him."

"I see. Thank you." She smiled at him. "I appreciate you coming by and warning me."

"Yes, well." Tugging on the collar of his sport shirt, he seemed uncomfortable now. "Since the curse comes from my family, it seemed the least I could do."

"Right. Thanks again." She held the door open, keeping her pleasant smile in place while he got in his car, waving until the dark sedan disappeared from view. When she turned to go back inside, she found her aunt standing in the foyer.

"What was that all about?" Wiping her hands on her apron, Marilyn frowned.

"He's just being a priest." Suddenly, Brie was tired. Tired of secrets, tired of lies. "Father Malcolm is afraid the Hunter curse is going to get me. He says I might have already brought it down on my head."

Her aunt gasped. "What?"

"By having Reed act as my Nya. I changed this morning, Aunt Marilyn. And Reed was with me."

Struck speechless, her aunt nodded.

"Don't worry." Brie kept her tone brisk. "I'm going to call Reed." She refused to show concern. Not until she had good reason.

"You don't seem too afraid."

"What do you expect me to do? Curl up in a ball in a corner, shaking from fear that each breath I take will be my last?" Brie smiled to take the sting off her words. "Have another panic attack? I'm not like that anymore, Aunt Marilyn. I've taken up a new motto. *No Fear.*"

"Yes, but what if Malcolm's right? What if Reed's relationship as your Nya has brought the curse upon you? What are you going to do?"

"I'll deal with the stupid curse, the only way I know how. I need to find out the reason it came into existence."

"Stupid? Don't underestimate the power of that thing. People have died because of that curse."

"Oh, I don't. I just find it odd that no one has tried to figure out the why. There's got to be a reason and, once that's discovered, a way to end it."

"I've been trying…" Aunt Marilyn sighed. "But there aren't enough hours in the day."

Brie jerked her hand toward Marilyn's library. "I guess I'd better get back to reading those old books. I've got a feeling all of this—stalker, curse and my mom's murder, are all tied together."

"How?"

"I don't know. But maybe somewhere in one of these books I might find an answer."

"I've never seen anything like that." Marilyn shook her head. "But just because I haven't, doesn't mean it couldn't be there. Go ahead and search. I'll come help you once I've finished in the kitchen."

Squaring her shoulders, Brie headed back to the library and picked up another book. She'd read another couple of hours, and then head back to Reed's.

She had a stalker to catch, after all.

Until she had concrete evidence that the damn curse could touch her, she refused to worry about that.

Chapter 14

Luckily, by the time Brie had to leave her aunt's to meet Reed for supper, she'd calmed down enough to think clearly. Going on the basis the curse was real, she didn't really know if she had been cursed—yet.

But if she took things a step further and assumed Father Malcolm was right, she could give in to the desire that consumed her, and make love to Reed.

Even thinking about that made her break out in a cold sweat. No Fear, she reminded herself. They were both consenting adults, denying themselves each other for the most unbelievable reason she'd ever heard.

Right then and there, she knew she was going to go for it. Still, she had no plan. Though she knew he wanted her as badly as she wanted him, she also knew she couldn't simply run up to him, throw her arms around him and ask him to make love to her.

Letting herself into Reed's house with her key and balancing a sack of groceries on her hip, she hummed as she made her way to the kitchen. Depositing her goodies on the counter, she flicked on the light and got to work. She'd been craving spaghetti and a good meal might help her think.

A short while later, she heard the garage door open.

When Reed walked in the room, head down while he sorted through the mail, her knees went weak.

"Hey," she said, soft-voiced and trembling with lust.

"Hey, yourself." He looked at her, his dark gaze full of indefinable emotion. "Smells great in here. What's all this?"

"I cooked spaghetti." She managed a breezy tone and carefree smile. "I hope you're hungry."

"Starving." His smile made her stomach clench.

"Did you talk to your uncle today?"

"I tried. We ended up playing phone tag all day. One of his messages said he planned to visit you. Did he ever make it?"

"Yes." She bit her lip. "We need to talk—"

"In a little bit, okay?" He held up his hand. "I'm starving. Do you mind if we eat first?"

At her nod, he stopped by the refrigerator and snagged a beer. "Let me change out of my uniform and we'll dig in."

When he returned, Brie suppressed her restlessness and they ate in a comfortable silence, with all the lights on. No soft mood music, nor glowing candlelight— Brie knew that would have been too obvious. If Reed was ever willingly going to make love to her, it would have to develop naturally, rather than as a result of a planned seduction.

He ate with obvious enjoyment, even going back for seconds. Then, when they'd both finished, he helped her carry the dishes to the sink and offered to wash them if she'd dry. Startled, but pleased, she agreed.

After the final dish had been dried she stretched. It was odd how warm and fuzzy such a simple act like washing dishes could make her feel. "It's warm in here. What's it like outside?"

"It's a beautiful night." He watched her closely, male appreciation in his lazy smile. "Want to go for a walk in the woods?"

Her pulse leaped at the thought. "Could we... That is, could I...?"

"Change? Certainly."

Impulsively she hugged him. The instant their bodies touched, she felt electrified, weak at the knees.

He pulled back first, his eyes haunted. "That wasn't a good idea." His voice sounded raspy, as shaky as she felt inside. Oh God, once she told him—would he see it as an open door, as she did?

"Reed, we seriously need to talk."

"Not now." Going to the back door, he held it open. She shook her head and slipped her hand into his. He tensed, then squeezed her fingers before releasing them. Not touching, they walked outside. With the soft grass underfoot, the chirping of crickets for music, and the heavy orb of the full moon silver in the dark sky, she couldn't have asked for a more perfect night.

When they reached the glade, she kept her gaze locked on his while she peeled off her clothes. Once naked, she lifted her arms to the sky and let her head fall back while she bathed in moonlight.

His harsh intake of breath was followed by the sound

of his zipper, then the rustle of his jeans as he pulled them off.

She wouldn't look, afraid to tempt herself too much. She wanted to change.

Dropping to all fours, digging her fingers in the clay earth, she let instinct take over. The change came easier this time, though her blood still boiled when her bones tugged and lengthened. Beside her, she sensed Reed doing the same.

Once she was wolf, she breathed deep, loving the myriad sharp scents she now detected.

With a yip, he tore past her. She let him get a good distance away, then she took off running. She ran as though she could purge the desire from her body, ran as though the exertion would cleanse her of need.

But if the curse was real, she knew she couldn't outrun it. She could only hope to outwit it.

Occasionally, she caught glimpses of another wolf. Reed, though he kept his distance, ran with her, watching. Always close.

When her sides heaved and her trembling legs felt as though they'd no longer support her, she dropped to her belly on the cool, damp earth and rolled. Panting, eyes closed, she let exhaustion claim her. Still wolf, finally, she slept.

Reed stood guard. In wolf form, he watched the woman he longed to take as mate, and ached. Finally, he lay down beside her, muzzle to muzzle, and kept watch. Finally, he dozed.

When a sound startled him awake, he woke as a human. Groggily he took stock, amazed. He was no longer wolf. Somehow, he'd changed without knowing, changed without effort, unconsciously while slumbering. This had never happened to him before, not once.

He glanced next to him, at Brie. She, too, had become human again, and still slumbered. Lying on the leaf-covered ground, creamy skin gilded with moonlight, he couldn't tear his eyes away. He'd never seen her look more beautiful or more desirable.

His. The thought came out of nowhere, slamming into him so hard he staggered. *Mate.*

"No," he muttered, though he argued with no one but himself. Mate meant… No. "She's not. She can't be."

"Reed?" She'd opened her eyes. Raising herself up on one elbow, completely unselfconscious in her nudity, she gave him a sleepy, slow smile that started him burning. "What time is it?"

He hadn't worn a watch. "I don't know." Dragging a hand through his hair, he stood and tried to turn away to hide his jutting arousal.

But she'd seen. "Please. Look at me." Her voice was smoky, inviting. Irresistible.

He made the mistake of glancing at her. Their gazes locked. She held out her arms, her perfect, nude body a temptation impossible to resist. He'd actually taken a step toward her without realizing before he pulled himself together and shook his head.

"No."

Ignoring him, she arched her back. "Make love to me."

His body reacted. He cursed. "I can't make love to you." His harsh words warred with his obvious need. "Not now, not ever."

Desire had darkened her eyes to the color of a stormy sea. When she dropped her gaze lower, he felt it exactly as if she'd touched him with her hand.

"We can," she insisted and, still on her knees, crossed the few feet that separated them.

Though he knew he should retreat, his feet felt rooted to the earth. When she reached him, she followed up her words with a bold caress that left him gasping.

He grabbed her hand, stilling her. "Brie, you're not listening. I know how the change affects you—all of us feel like we've had a shot of adrenaline when we change back to human. But that alters nothing between us. Don't you see—" His words were cut off when she wiggled closer, pressing her naked body against his, raising herself up and rubbing against him like an affectionate cat, her breasts full and enticing against his erection. Though he still held her hand, she used her body in other ways, driving his protests completely from his mind.

His mate. Brie. The ultimate temptress.

But he was stronger than his desire. He had to resist. Had no choice, even if his body had other ideas.

"Brie, stop." Even as he spoke, he surged against her, hard, ready. In torment.

Without taking her gaze from his, she licked her lips. "I want to feel you inside me more than anything. But first, I want to taste you."

Hell hounds—he closed his eyes, fighting the urge to push himself into her mouth. The image of her full lips wrapped around him nearly made him spill his seed right then and there.

"It would be the same thing." He heard his own voice, seeming to come from a long ways off. Struggling to focus on her through the haze of desire, he swallowed. "You'd be cursed. We can't."

"Would it? Does the curse specifically say you can't have sex?"

"Relationship," he ground out. "Any woman involved in a relationship with a Hunter male is doomed."

"Then I'm already doomed." She reared her head back, making him look at her face. Though she spoke lightly, her expression was serious. "When your uncle Malcolm came to see me earlier today, he wanted to warn me. He said when you acted as my Nya, we entered a relationship. He said I was already cursed."

At her words, he went utterly still, though his sex still throbbed. "Already...no. It's not possible."

"Yes, it is." Her quiet insistence hummed with an undercoating of desire. "Whether we make love or not, we still have a relationship, Reed. It's there. I'm cursed."

"But—"

"No buts." She laid a kiss against his belly, making him quiver. "If I'm already cursed, at least give me this. Don't deny us this pleasure. There's no longer a reason not to make love."

"No longer a..." He closed his eyes, swaying. "I didn't think of that. I should've known, I...." He lost his train of thought as she lowered her mouth over the long, hard length of him.

His head swam. Both from desire and her revelation. Then she moved again and he forgot to even think.

"All this time..." he managed. "Why didn't you...?"

She lifted her mouth from him and kissed him full on the lips. "Pay attention. I'm telling you now. Make love to me, Reed. Mate with me. Be my mate."

Before he could answer, before he could think, she lifted herself over him and plunged down hard, sheathing him so completely he lost the last shred of his already frayed control.

They were mates, in every way that mattered. Body to body. Heart to heart. Soul to soul.

Later, holding her in his arms, he thought he'd be content to die right now, right here, having known this woman. Though he'd loved Teresa dearly, he'd never felt this meshing, like two halves of the same soul, finally joined.

He'd finally found his true mate.

And, because of the curse that followed him, she was now slated to die.

No way.

He had to figure out how to keep that from happening. Even if he had to give his own life to do it.

Back at the house, Reed headed into the kitchen to make a pot of coffee. In her small bathroom, Brie washed up, wetting her short hair to make it behave, and brushing her teeth. When she rejoined him in the kitchen, she saw he'd done the same.

Fixing herself a mug, she took the chair across from him and hoped the coffee's warmth could dispel the growing chilliness inside her.

"What now?" He watched her over the rim of his cup. "What do we do now?"

"We go on as before." She made her voice firm. "We still need answers. Now there are two things I want to investigate—my mother's death and your family curse."

His jaw tightened. "Brie…"

She ignored him. "So starting with the first. We haven't made much progress in learning anything new about my mother's killer."

A shadow crossed his face, gone so quickly she wasn't sure she'd even seen it. He nodded. "I know.

Sometimes when so much time has passed, the trail has grown too cold to follow."

"I have an idea." She chose her words carefully. "We need to bring the stalker to us. Let me act as bait. Once he bites, reel him in."

"Hell, no." He hit the table edge with the flat of his hand, causing her coffee to splash out of her mug. "That would be inviting death. Not gonna happen."

"Inviting death? Or inviting the curse?"

"They're one and the same."

"Reed, he's been quiet lately. He hasn't made a move in days—"

"He shot out my window."

"Yes, but my point is, he's gone dormant. If we want to catch him, we need to draw him out."

"Absolutely not."

"Reed—"

Pushing himself up so suddenly his chair crashed to the ground, he grabbed her. Hauled her up against him and kissed her, long and deep, and thoroughly.

When he finally lifted his mouth from hers, she was limp and weak with desire.

"Don't talk about that again." Reed touched his nose to hers. "That's too dangerous. I can't lose you, not now. Not ever."

She heaved a sigh, knowing she'd have to wait for another time to try to convince him. "Fine," she said. "What now? Any other ideas?"

His clear gaze was direct and full of warmth. "It couldn't hurt to go over everything again." He pointed at the counter, where the manila case files were neatly stacked.

"I've gone over them until I can't see straight."

"All right. Then let's talk about the notes your mother received. How much do you remember about what they said? It'd be better if we could go over them one by one, but since they were stolen…"

"I read them enough to memorize parts of them."

"Good. Tell me about them. We're looking for clues." Pen poised, he watched her expectantly.

"They started off nice. Friendly. Lots of compliments—she was beautiful, she was smart, stuff like that. But even then I got a feeling of…creepiness from them."

"Go on."

"After a few of those, the letter writer upped the intensity. Still complimentary, but now in a more sexual way. Mentioning her breasts, her lips…"

She took a deep breath. "Those must have pissed her off or something. She took some sort of action. Because the next letter refers to something she did. Maybe she had someone pay the letter writer a visit, maybe threaten him."

"Aha." Reed tapped his pen on the table. "We've got to find that person, the one she sent, and find out who he went to see."

"How? The letters never mentioned a name."

"Let's think for a minute. If you were scared and mad and didn't want to worry your husband, who would you go to for help?"

"A relative. My father or my brother, if I had one."

"If you didn't have a father or brother? What about your priest?"

"Definitely. It has to be him. Who else could she go to? Are you thinking she had Father Malcolm pay the guy a visit?"

"It's possible." He shrugged. "My uncle might be a

man of the cloth now, but he was a linebacker in high school. He's a big man."

Brie shook her head. "I asked him if she'd come to him, told him anything. He said conversations made in confession are personal, and he couldn't share them, not even twenty-two years later."

"I think the church has unbreakable rules about that."

"But if my life's in danger…"

"That might be reason enough." Reed's expression was grim. "He might be willing to break a rule or two."

"Okay, so we talk to Father Malcolm. I still think you need to visit Eldon Brashear again. I'm positive he knows more than he's telling."

"Maybe. Monday, I'll go. Alone. At least I have a chance he'll talk to me if I'm by myself."

"True." She conceded the point. "I'd also like to continue looking through my aunt's library."

He smiled. "Still thinking you might stumble across something about the curse?"

"I am." Leaning forward, she kissed him full on the lips. "And I think that's another area where your uncle Malcolm knows more than he lets on."

"Really?" Reed's dark brows rose as he kissed her back. "What makes you say that? I think he's told us— his own family—all he knows. It is our curse, after all."

"I don't think so. He hinted one time about mysteries and the church."

"Strange." He smiled. "But on the family curse, I know for certain if he knew anything helpful, he'd reveal it. He hates that curse more than anyone."

"I really like your uncle. He's the closest thing I'll have to a father, now that my real dad is gone."

Lifting her fingers to his mouth, he kissed the

knuckle of each one. "He likes you, too. Maybe even like a daughter. Or a niece-in-law."

She went still at his words. Then, looking away, decided it would be best not to acknowledge them at all. They had way too much to do before they could even begin talks of a possible future together.

She pushed herself out of the chair and carried her empty coffee cup to the sink. "We'd better get started if we're going to visit your uncle. The day is half-gone."

"It's Sunday!" he protested. "Don't you think a priest is awfully busy on Sundays?"

"Yes, but services are over and everyone's had time to have Sunday lunch. By the way, I would think you'd be a regular churchgoer, with your uncle being the priest and all. Why don't you ever go to Mass?"

His mouth a tight line, he looked away. "I swore never to set foot in that church again, as long as the bell remained unbroken. And I haven't, not since Teresa's funeral."

She regarded him steadily. "Do you want to wait outside while I go get him?"

"Now? Today?"

"Sure, why not. The evening service won't be for hours. This is a perfect time to ask your uncle Malcolm about my mother."

Half an hour later they pulled up in front of the church.

Brie waited while Reed killed the engine. "Are you coming with me?"

"I can't let you go alone, now can I?" Opening his door, Reed climbed out. After helping her down, he took her arm, escorting her up the walk.

"Do you really think he'll talk to us?"

"Who knows? We can only try."

Inside, the church was deserted, quiet and dark, as though slumbering in the midday heat. Only the candles flickering in the back provided movement.

The door separating the rectory from the classrooms was closed. Smiling down at her, Reed knocked on the door.

The door swung open. A disheveled Father Malcolm peered at them with red-rimmed eyes. He looked as though they'd awakened him from a nap.

"Sorry to bother you." Reed stepped forward. "But we need to talk to you about something that's fairly urgent."

"Certainly, certainly," the older man muttered. "Come in, have a seat. Would you two give me a moment or two to clean myself up?"

"Sure." Reed pulled out a chair at the kitchen table for Brie.

Malcolm stumbled into the bathroom and closed the door. A moment later they heard water running.

"I feel horrible about waking him." Brie popped up from her chair, fighting the urge to fidget, and dropped back down.

"I do too, but this is important. The more I think about it, the more logical it sounds that Elizabeth would have come to my uncle Malcolm for help."

"I don't understand why she wouldn't let her husband take care of it."

"Of course she couldn't. She loved him." Reed stroked her short hair. "Your father was human. If her stalker was Pack and she knew it, your father would have been no match for him."

She couldn't argue with that logic.

A moment later Father Malcolm emerged from the bathroom.

"Sorry about that. The services this morning seemed unusually…difficult and I've been feeling a bit run down. Hopefully I'm not coming down with something."

"I hope not." Reed indicated the chair next to him. "Have a seat."

"This couldn't have waited?" The priest stifled a yawn. "I really am tired."

"We'll be out of your way in a minute." He waited until Malcolm was seated before continuing. "We have reason to believe Elizabeth Beswick was being stalked."

"Brie mentioned she believed her mother was murdered. I can tell you now, she took her own life. I am certain of that." Looking from one to the other, Father Malcolm rubbed his eyes. "If this is what you wanted to talk to me about, quite honestly, it could have waited."

"That's not all." Reed leaned forward, touching his uncle's arm. "We really need to know if Elizabeth ever came to you and asked you to speak to someone, or expressed worry or fear about anyone?"

Lips compressed in a tight line, the priest looked down at his hands. "You know I can't—"

"This is a matter of life and death. If you care at all about Brie, help me protect her."

"The church is very strict on this. Such matters are confidential."

"Confession is." Reed stood, jamming his hands into his pockets. "But Elizabeth wouldn't have been confessing, *Father* Malcolm. You were her priest. She came to you for help. That's different."

Malcolm glared at him. Reed glared back.

Brie held her breath, waiting.

"I don't know…"

"Do you want Brie's death on your hands?" Jaw

tight, Reed voice was full of controlled fury. "Is that what you want?"

"Of course not."

"Then tell us. Did Elizabeth Beswick ever come to you and ask you to speak to someone who was threatening her?"

"Very well." Malcolm pinched his nose. His hands shook. "If you must know, Elizabeth was very afraid of Eldon Brashear. She said he wouldn't leave her alone, even though she was happily married."

Eldon Brashear. Exactly as she'd thought all along.

"And Eldon has threatened Scott Wells, several times. Scott came to me, wanting to discuss…" Malcolm's words trailed off, as if he was afraid he'd said too much.

"Discuss what?" Reed asked. "I know how Scott is, and he wouldn't take any threat lying down. The man's probably got an arsenal out there in the woods."

"Protecting himself. He was afraid Eldon would try to kill him."

Numb, Brie could barely speak as they said their goodbyes. The priest appeared severely shaken, his conscience at war with his vows.

"You did the right thing." Reed clapped him on the shoulder on the way out. "What you've told us might save Brie's life."

Brie nodded woodenly. Only when they were safely buckled in to Reed's truck, was she able to articulate her emotions. "If he killed my mother…"

"If, Brie." But Reed's face was as grim as her thoughts. "Remember, he's innocent until proven guilty."

"I know, but if he's the one who's been stalking me… He's the one who killed my mother."

"I can promise you this. If Eldon Brashear killed Elizabeth and passed it off as suicide, he'll be punished to the full extent of the law. I can promise you that."

"That's not enough," she cried, rage and grief warring with the awful numbness. "He deprived me of so much…."

"Let me elaborate." Reed's tone was savage as he gripped the wheel and drove. "I'm not speaking of human law. Pack law would apply in this instance. And Pack law dictates an automatic death sentence."

Chapter 15

When they pulled up to Eldon's house, Reed left the truck idling.

"Are you going to arrest him?"

He sighed. "Can't. We don't have any evidence linking him with any crime. All I can do is question him and hope he confesses, which is highly unlikely."

"Oh." Brie surveyed the place doubtfully. "Do you think he's home?"

Glancing back at the house, he saw the front window curtain twitch, letting him know they were being watched. "He's home. I want you to stay in the truck while I talk to him. I'll stay on the front porch, never out of your sight."

She nodded.

When Reed knocked on the door, Eldon made him wait. He counted to twenty, and knocked again. This time, the door swung open and Eldon scowled at him.

"What do you want?" He peered past Reed, glaring at the truck. "And if it's about her mama, you can forget it. There's some things better left unsaid."

"Before she died, I've learned Elizabeth Beswick sent someone to talk to you, to warn you away from her."

Eldon grunted, chewing furiously. "Your informant, whoever it is, is lyin'."

Reed wanted to tell him his informant was a priest and that priests didn't lie, but couldn't. "Come on, Eldon. I know all about it."

"No one never talked to me 'bout that woman." Eldon spat a wad of chewing tobacco on a bush next to Reed. "Had no reason to. I never bothered her. Once we were through, we were through."

He folded his arms and glared at Reed, darting occasional fuming looks at Brie.

Finally, there was nothing to do but leave.

Climbing back in the truck, Reed met Brie's inquisitive look with a grim shake of his head. "That was a complete waste of time. He admits nothing, knows nothing, and won't budge an inch."

"Then what are we going to do?"

"We've got to find evidence, hard evidence. Or we don't have a chance in hell of bringing him in."

Once back at the police station, Reed waved to Tammy and shepherded Brie back to his office. He closed the door.

"I'm going to run another check on Eldon's criminal history, even though the first one came back clean. Sometimes there's a glitch." Punching in his password, he accessed the online data system. "And I'll get Scott Wells's records, too, while I'm at it."

"Why?"

"Just because my uncle talked to Eldon doesn't mean Eldon's the killer."

She snorted. "I still think you ought to at least consider letting me try and flush him out. It appears he's taking a break."

"No." Reed didn't even look up from his computer. "I won't risk you. Not for anything."

She leaned back in her chair and crossed her arms. "I want to find my mother's killer, you know that."

"She wouldn't want you to die for it."

"It won't come to that."

He swiveled his chair around to face her. "You don't know that. Sure, it appears this guy has gone underground, but you never know what might set him off. If he's a shifter, and he probably is, you'll be no match for him."

"I've changed."

"Twice. He'll have been doing it his entire life. No, better we concentrate on figuring out what happened. What was different to this guy about Marilyn?"

Now he had her attention. "What do you mean?"

"She got letters, just like your mother's. But he never threatened her. You said her letters stopped when she married your Uncle Albert."

"That's what she said."

"But your mother's didn't. Why not?"

Brie frowned. "That is weird. If I remember right, when my mother got engaged, the letter writer seemed to grow more desperate."

"Unlike Marilyn's." He stood. "I think we need to pay your aunt a quick visit. I want to take a look at her letters."

Brie called ahead. When they arrived at her aunt's house, Marilyn was waiting, a neat, rubber-banded, bundle of letters in hand and a worried expression on her broad face. She brought them iced tea and watched silently while they settled in at her kitchen table to read.

"What about Edie?" Reed asked, after finishing. "Brie says she asked Edie and never got any. That doesn't make sense." He flicked his finger at the rubber band, popping it. "If this guy is targeting Beswick women, why exclude her?"

Marilyn waggled her plump finger at him. "Reed, you know Edie's adopted. She's not a Beswick, she's from another Pack out West. Most everyone in town knows that."

"Adopted?" Brie looked from her aunt to Reed. "No one ever told me. Even Edie herself has never mentioned it."

"She had no reason. She's one of us now. She's been here her entire life. Her parents died in a house fire when she was two. Albert and I took her in and raised her. We made the whole thing formal the year she started kindergarten."

"I didn't know that." Reed shrugged. "I must have been a kid when that happened."

"Well." Aunt Marilyn shrugged. "Maybe only the older folks remember it now. But Edie's never been bothered by these letters." She took a deep breath and looked him full in the face. "I believe that's because Edie doesn't carry Beswick blood."

Reading over the letters again, Brie shook her head. "They might have been carbon copies of my mother's earlier ones. They're eerily similar in tone."

"Do you really think Brie's in danger?" Hands on ample hips, Marilyn asked her question in a forceful voice, like she was daring danger to just try and get past her. "Whoever wrote these letters never did anything to me."

Reed caught her eye and Brie nodded. Might as well tell her aunt everything.

"Yes," he said simply. "Yes, I do." He told her what they'd worked out so far.

"Then you need to leave town, honey." Marilyn rounded on Brie. "No sense in putting yourself in harm's way. Maybe it's time for you to go back to Colorado."

"No." Brie shook her head. "I've spent my entire life running, until now. I've been alone, except for my dad, and he's gone now. I refuse to let this stalker run me off. This is my new life, my town. My family."

"What about the curse?" Reed spoke, surprising her. "If leaving will get you away from the curse, I think you should do what your aunt suggests, and go."

"No fear. I'm not going anywhere."

Reed exchanged a long look with Marilyn, then looked at Brie. "At least consider it."

"Sorry," she told him, even though he knew she wasn't.

That night, they ran in the forest side by side. They played like puppies, crashing into each other, rolling on the ground, shaking leaves from their fur. She learned the fine art of gentle biting, the quick nip that felt playful rather than brutal, and the way to tuck her tail under herself so she could slink about in the undergrowth.

As her wolf self, she was stronger, more confident. More certain that everything would work out, no matter what.

Finally, the fear and tension and stress run out of her, she skidded to a stop and, panting, changed from wolf to woman. In human form, she got to her feet as Reed padded into the clearing, watching as he, too, shifted.

As before, sparkles of light danced around him, making the actual transformation a thing of mystical magic rather than horror.

Fully human, he raised his head and met her gaze. Hunger had darkened his eyes so they appeared black. He reached for her. She met him halfway. Sinking together to the ground, they made love with a desperate urgency, as frantic as if this time would be their last.

Sated, they slept again in the woods, with only the creatures of the forest as witnesses.

At sunrise, he woke her with a touch. She rose and still wordless, they padded back to the house together. Once there, Brie headed for the shower, supposing Reed would do the same. When she emerged from her room a half hour later in clean clothes with her hair dried, Reed had already left for work.

She decided to head over to her aunt's library and see if she could learn anything else about shape-shifters or the curse. She still believed a combination of things had led to her mother's death. She wanted to know the same things the killer knew. Only then would she have a chance of stopping him before he got angry enough to try and hurt her or worse.

Aunt Marilyn was on her way out to a Ladies' Club meeting when Brie arrived.

"Help yourself, hon. Just make sure and lock up when you're finished." A quick hug, a peck on the cheek, and Aunt Marilyn took off in her huge, blue Cadillac. Brie waited until the car disappeared around the corner before going in to the house and locking the door.

Though she'd promised not to be alone, she knew Reed was only a phone call away. And part of her, the stubborn, optimistic part, still clung to the notion of drawing the stalker out. Was he hanging back—waiting?

Brie didn't want that. She wanted to find the s.o.b. and clear her mother's name. She wanted answers, a way to break the curse, a reason for everything. Maybe, she thought with a grin, her need to have everything neatly tied up came from such a rootless childhood. Once everything was compartmentalized, in its place, she'd feel more secure.

But for now, she instinctively felt, in much the same way Reed could sometimes "hear" her thoughts, the stalker and the curse were tied together. The answer just might be in one of these old books, waiting for her to find it. Problem was, there were hundreds of them. Would she be able to find it in time?

An hour later, Brie looked up from the page, stretched and glanced longingly out the window which looked into the backyard. Though outside the weather was perfect—cloudless blue sky and balmy, summer breeze—Aunt Marilyn still refused to allow any of the books out of the library room. Brie wasn't supposed to even carry them onto the back deck. If Brie wanted to learn Pack history, and maybe glean snippets about the Hunter's curse, she had to read here. Her aunt claimed they were too ancient, too valuable, to risk exposure to the elements.

Carefully placing the three books she'd skimmed back on the bookshelf, this time Brie deliberately looked for the oldest books. Her aunt had designated an entire section inside a closed bookcase. Some of the covers were dusty, some so old the material appeared cracked and faded. She chose four of these and carried them back to her seat. With her fresh stack of books on the table in front of her, Brie glanced once more at the tempting sunshine before opening the top book, which appeared to have been written in the late seventeenth century. It was written in a style reminiscent of colonial times. Elaborate script accompanied the overblown wording, making it difficult to read. When she caught herself yawning for the third time, she put down the book and glanced at her watch.

Unsurprised to note that barely twenty minutes had passed, she sighed. She itched to call Reed, just to hear his voice, but recognized that longing as foolish.

Cracking the book open again, she struggled through a few more pages. Nothing here. Closing the cover carefully, she slid it across the table and reached for the next one.

The doorbell rang, startling her. Peering though the peephole, she saw Reed standing on the front porch. Talk about reading her mind!

"Hey." He smiled when she opened the door, his eyes glowing. "I thought you might be hungry. Want to go get a bite to eat?"

She laughed, feeling warm and fuzzy and happier to see him than she should. "I was just thinking about calling you. I'd love to. Come in. Give me a second to close things up."

Motioning him inside, she led him back to the library. "Let me put these books back in order and we'll go."

"Great. I've got to stop by the house and pick up a set of keys to the warehouse. One of my guys needs to retrieve some old evidence from a case that's coming up for trial this week."

"Works for me."

When they pulled up to the house, Reed cursed. A large, manila envelope had been taped to his front door. Brie's name was scrawled across the front in blood-red marker. Brie had received yet another letter.

"Looks like he didn't go away after all." Reed shook his head, pocketing the keys. "Wonder what he sent you this time."

"I'm almost afraid to open it."

He glanced at her, expression grim. "I'll do it."

Together they climbed the steps, both of them careful to continually scan the yard. When they reached the front door, Reed plucked the envelope off and ripped open one end.

He swore again, his tone savage. "In the house," he ordered, unlocking the door and pushing it open. "Now."

Once inside, he secured the deadbolt before looking at her. The fury she saw in his face took her breath away.

"What is it?" She tried to look, but he shielded her. "Reed, let me see."

Wordlessly, he handed her several pictures. Photos of her and Reed naked, kissing in the forest. Starkly graphic photos of them intertwined, in the seconds before they'd made love. And more.

"Good Lord." Brie swallowed, feeling sick. "Last night when we… He must have been watching us."

Eyes blazing murder, Reed nodded. "When I get my hands on him…"

She knew the feeling. "What does the letter say?"

Opening the note, he positioned the paper so they could read it together. It had been typed on the same ancient typewriter with the faint *e*.

"We've pissed him off now. He's gone straight to threats, says I have to change my ways or die."

His cell phone rang. "Hunter here," he barked. He listened a moment, then clicked the phone closed. "That was Peter Rasinski. I've got to go. They found Scott Wells dead. It looks like the stalker got him. And the stalker must be Pack too—Scott's body looks like it's been mauled by a wolf."

"But…" She swallowed, then lifted her chin. "I thought only silver bullets or fire…" citing one of the books she'd read "…could kill a shifter."

"True. After Scott Wells's jugular was ripped open, while he lay bleeding, the stalker must have changed back and shot him. He died with a silver bullet lodged in his heart."

"I'm going with you."

"Of course you are." He kissed her, a quick, hard press of his mouth on hers. "No way are you staying alone now."

The M.E. had already ordered the body transported to the morgue. Reed had Brie wait in his truck, doors locked, when they arrived. As soon as Reed checked in, an autopsy would be performed. According to Peter, Scott Wells had been brutally mangled, his jugular so badly torn that his head had practically been ripped from his body. Reed didn't want her to witness the evidence of so much bloody violence.

He told her he'd also sent Greg to pick up Eldon Brashear and bring him in for questioning.

Two uniformed deputies, state police, both of them, met him at the door. One of them, young and apparently new to police work, looked green around the gills, like he'd been clutching a toilet for the last half hour. If Wells was torn up as bad as Peter had indicated, Reed couldn't blame him.

As he walked down the long hall toward the examining room, his radio crackled. A second later, his cell phone began to ring. He opted for the radio. It was dispatch, sounding hysterical.

Eldon Brashear's home was on fire. Eldon himself was nowhere to be found.

Barely sparing poor Scott's body a look, Reed ordered Pete to remain there to get the autopsy report. He apologized to the M.E., an older woman named Celia, and took off at a run.

When he got to the truck, he kept his voice low as he filled Brie in. "This is all coming to a head. I'm going to take you to stay with my uncle until I get back. The church will be safe. The stalker won't look there."

She shook her head. "I want to go with you."

"You can't. This most likely will get bloody, before it's all over. You're a civilian. If you got hurt in the middle of this, all hell would break loose with the media, the state, everything."

"Then don't let me get hurt."

Her faith in him both moved and astounded him. "Brie, there's a crazed killer on a rampage. He's been stalking you. He stalked your mother. He killed her. Who do you think he wants to kill next? There's no way in hell I'm putting you in the line of danger."

She sighed. "Then I'll wait at the church. Father Malcolm always makes me feel safe."

"Good." One hand on the steering wheel, he opened his cell and punched up the speed dial for the church. "I need to call him and fill him in on what's going on."

His radio crackled before he could complete the call.

It was Tammy, asking where he was. The media had gathered at the police station, wanting answers. Quickly he filled her in on what to say—mostly "no comment"—and what he was going to do. He'd be there as soon as he could.

The second he punched the off button, his cell phone rang. Uncle Malcolm had seen his number on the caller I.D.

In a few short sentences, Reed told him what had happened.

"I'd be glad to keep watch over Brie." Malcolm's voice, as always, was soothing. "I've located old high school yearbooks with her mother in them. She'll enjoy seeing them. Bring her by."

When he hung up, Reed felt calmer. "That's settled. You'll be in good hands and out of harm's way."

Once they reached town, they parked in the side street by the church and walked in the side door rather than the front. Sunlight beamed through the stained glass windows, coloring the rich wood of the pews in vibrant blues, reds and yellows. As always, the atmosphere in the sanctuary filled Reed with a sense of rightful belonging, as if he'd come home. He missed attending Mass more than he'd ever admit.

Brie's low-heeled sandals clicked as they walked back to the rectory.

Father Malcolm stepped into the hallway before they reached his door. "Welcome," he said, smiling his gentle smile. Turning to Reed, he clapped him on the back. "Go take care of business, my boy. I'll watch out for Brie."

Reed nodded. Unable to leave without touching her, he gave Brie a swift kiss on the lips. "Stay safe."

"Be careful," she whispered.

The priest watched, concern plain in his face, his obvious dismay due to the curse. "Reed—"

Reed's radio crackled again. "Got to run." He took off at a jog, praying he could find Eldon Brashear before he harmed anyone else.

Watching Reed leave, Brie shivered as she pictured him facing an enraged Eldon Brashear, armed and savagely dangerous.

"He'll be fine." Father Malcolm patted her arm.

"I certainly hope so." Forcing a smile, she glanced back toward the rectory. "Now how about we take a look at those yearbooks you mentioned?"

"Not here." He glanced around the empty sanctuary as though someone might overhear them. "I think we should go for a drive, get out of here."

"Leave?" She stared at him in disbelief. "With Eldon Brashear running around looking for me?"

"Brie, I can't lock this church. That would be like denying the parish access to God. If Eldon shows up here, I don't know how I could protect you."

What he said made sense. Still, Reed had asked her to stay here. "I don't know…"

"We'll keep moving, stay on the run. I was thinking we'd head north, away from town and from Eldon's."

She hesitated.

"I've promised to keep you safe." His voice earnest, his gaze pleading. "I take my word seriously. I don't want him to get you, Brie."

Still hesitant, she studied him.

"Would you like to call Reed and ask him?" He held out a cell phone. "Go ahead."

"I don't want to bother him." With a sigh, she gave in. "All right. Let's go."

As he headed toward the same side door she'd entered, she thought of something. "Father?"

He turned, his black cassock swirling. "Yes?"

"Do you have a gun?" At his startled expression, she explained. "You never know. We might need it to defend ourselves. Better safe than sorry."

"I do have one." He hurried back toward the rectory. "Let me get it."

"Make sure you have silver bullets," she called after him.

When he returned, he took her arm. "Let's go. My car is parked out here."

His dark sedan looked priestly—and safe. They drove north through town, the road steadily climbing.

"Here we are." The priest turned his ancient Buick down a nearly obscure dirt track that reminded her of Scott Wells's driveway, but worse. Tree limbs scraped the car's sides as they drove slowly to the forest.

"Where are we going?" Mildly alarmed, she glanced around. "I thought you wanted to drive."

The priest smiled his serene, comforting smile. "This is a place I felt you should see. This is Hollowood Heights. It used to be the traditional wedding meadow, where all the Pack wedding ceremonies were held, up until twenty or so years ago."

"What happened to change that?" she asked, afraid she already knew.

"Your mother's death." One hand on the door handle, he gave her a slow smile. "And then, twenty years later, Reed's wife Teresa died here, too. Same gun, same silver bullet."

Brie's blood turned to ice. "Father Malcolm?" she said, incredulous. "You're the killer?"

He ignored her, holding out his hand. "Come on, Brie Beswick. I want to show you the place where your mother died."

Chapter 16

Shaking his head, Reed open his cell phone and stared at the small screen. Parked down the road from the fire trucks and the smoldering ruins that had been Eldon's place, he couldn't shake the sense that something was wrong with Brie.

Eldon was missing, ostensibly after slaughtering Scott Wells. Somehow, like the letters and the painting, he couldn't see Eldon committing such a horrific act. And, while he'd readily admit he didn't like the man, Eldon didn't seem like a murderer.

Then who…

He dialed her number.

She answered on the fifth ring, sounding peeved. "Reed? Yes, I'm still alive," she said, instead of hello. "Why would you imagine I'd be anything but safe? I'm with your uncle Malcolm." She sounded extremely agitated.

Reed's internal alarm went off, super-strength. "Brie, you sound weird. What's going on? Are you still at the church?"

"No," she said, her voice shaking. "I can't meet you for dinner tonight, Reed. Even if you did want to propose, that's not the place."

"Propose? What?" She wasn't making sense. "Brie, are you trying to give me a clue?"

"Yes. I'm sorry, but I'm busy. I can't talk now. Gotta go." She hung up on him.

Brie was in danger. The curse. The stalker. Screw the curse. The curse would have to roll over his dead body before he'd let it take her.

Determined, he snapped his phone closed and started his truck. Gunning the motor, he flipped on his lights and siren and sped off for the church.

"No." Brie shrank back against the door. While she stared at the priest, she tried to plan her escape. "I have no desire to see the place where my mother died."

"Yes, you do. You need closure."

Until she could come up with a decent plan, she needed to stall him. "Closure? My mother died when I was a small child. I had closure a long time ago. Why would you think I need that now?"

"Obviously you do. You can't let her death go. Having Reed reopen the investigation! Come on, now. It's been twenty-two years, my dear. Time to move on. Obtain closure. Once and for all." He laughed, the sound sending chills up her spine.

Father Malcolm was insane. And she knew insanity was much more dangerous than simple malice.

Another thought occurred to her. Since she was only

part shifter, could she be killed by traditional means? Or were silver bullets or fire the only way to end her life, too?

Either way, she needed to escape him. She could cover a lot more ground as a wolf. Her only hope would be to change and run for it. Of course, he might shoot at her, with the gun she'd insisted he bring along, or he'd change too. She was hoping he'd do the latter, as she thought since she was younger, she could outrun him.

Still new to changing, she'd have to make sure she chose the perfect opportunity; otherwise he'd be on her before she'd completed the change.

Her cell phone rang. She glanced at Malcolm.

"Who?"

She looked at the phone. "Reed. He promised to call me after he found Eldon Brashear."

"Answer it," Malcolm snarled. "Make small talk. Placate him. But be very, very careful what you say."

He watched her closely while she had a one-sided conversation with Reed. He'd been able to occasionally hear her thoughts. She willed him to understand her clues. When she closed the phone, it was with the knowledge that Reed would be trying to get to her.

"Very nice." The priest smiled. "You sounded ordinary, not at all afraid. I'm proud of you."

If he only knew… Should she try to run now? Or wait for a better opportunity? She decided to wait. *Stall him.* "I want to know why. Why Beswick women? Why did you kill my mother?"

Malcolm watched her closely, the way a wild animal watches prey. She realized the most important thing was not to show fear.

When he didn't answer, she repeated her question. "Why did you kill my mother?"

"She was my mate. She alone could break that damnable curse. But she refused."

The curse. She'd always suspected Malcolm knew more about it than he'd said. "You know how to end the curse?"

"Yes." Making an odd little twitch, he smiled. "The church has archived all the truly old books that refer to the curse. I made it my lifetime's goal to discover how to end the terrible hold it has on my family. And I did."

He grabbed her, pulled her close. "That's what I'm trying to do, here today, with you. In the traditional wedding meadow of our people. End the curse."

"What?" She fought not to recoil from him. "End the curse? How?"

He took a deep breath. "Marry me, Brie. Become my wife and end the curse."

"You're already married. To the Church."

"I will renounce my vows. Before you, before God, in the sacred meadow."

Brie couldn't help glancing at the sky. Any minute she expected lightning to snake down and strike him. When it didn't, she opened her door and got out. "Let me think about it," she said. She dropped to the ground, beginning the change.

He got out after her. "Brie?" he said. He came around the front of his car the instant the change began. "What are you doing? Stop!"

He was too late.

Wolf now, she took off running.

Reed pulled up at the church with a screech of tires. Though he didn't see Uncle Malcolm's ancient Buick, he bounded up the steps and checked the inside. The church was empty.

He tore back to the rectory, glancing in the darkened classrooms as he ran.

A quick sweep of his uncle's rooms showed they were deserted. No sign of his uncle Malcolm or Brie.

Where the hell were they?

Brie had said something about a proposal. A clue.

Suddenly, he remembered Hollowood Heights—the place her mother had died. Once, the meadow had been the traditional wedding site.

She was there. But with whom? And what had happened to his uncle?

He knew he'd find out. He could only hope he wasn't too late.

He drove like a crazed man. Once he turned on the old rutted road, he flicked off his sirens and flashing lights, knowing he'd see no other traffic out here.

He was rewarded when he spotted Malcolm's vehicle parked in the old clearing off the road. Years ago, this had been a gravel parking lot, but disuse and lack of interest had let the forest reclaim it.

He brought his truck to a stop behind Malcolm's car, intentionally blocking him in.

Now to find Brie and make sure she was safe.

He'd barely gone three feet into the underbrush when he saw a gray wolf, sides heaving, loping toward the trees on the other side of the meadow. Once he reached the edge of the forest, he dropped to the ground and began to change.

Uncle Malcolm.

Reed started forward. The hair on the back of his neck rose. "Uncle Malcolm," he called. "Where's Brie?"

His uncle rose and, reaching into the underbrush, yanked on his cassock. As Reed ran toward him, he saw a glint of metal as Malcolm pulled a gun.

"Don't come any closer," the priest ordered.

"You?" Recoiling, Reed stared in disbelief. "You're my only family. You've been like a father to me."

"What I do, I do for the good of our family."

"What?" Reed took a step toward him.

"Don't come any closer." Malcolm sighted the gun. "It's loaded with silver bullets."

Reed froze. "Where's Brie?"

"My bride?" Malcolm smiled.

"You're married to the Church." Reed kept his voice level. "Brie's mine. My mate. If you so much as harmed one hair on her head…"

"Harmed her? If anything harmed her, our curse would have done so. Like her mother before her, she refused to do what was necessary to end it," Malcolm snarled. "Our ancestors would have used my name as a blessing. No one would ever have forgotten me if she'd done as I asked. Now, I have to kill her."

Just like that, with those words, Reed knew his uncle was insane. How long he'd been so, Reed didn't know and right now, didn't care. He had to find Brie. "For the last time, where is she?"

Malcolm continued as though he hadn't heard him. "Like Brie, Elizabeth had it within her power to destroy the curse. I gave her a chance, a choice, the same one I gave Brie today. A Beswick must, of her own free will, wed a Hunter. Only then will the curse be ended. Only then will our family be free."

Keeping his face expressionless, Reed's mind whirled. He had two choices—draw his gun and hope he shot faster, or jump him. If he let the older man tell his story, he might be able to take him unaware. Knock his legs from under him, disarm him and cuff him.

Deciding to try the second, he cocked his head. "No one knows the story of our curse. Our family searched for years. No one ever found it."

"I did. In one of the church's ancient books. Oldest story in the universe. One of our ancestors raped a Beswick. At least, that's what the books call it. He was a priest, a man of God. Like me. Naturally, he wanted to keep their little affair a secret. When he learned she was with child, he killed her and her unborn babe."

Reed made a sound of disgust, keeping watch for the moment to attack.

His expression intense, Malcolm smiled. "In addition to being Pack, this Beswick woman was also a powerful witch. As she lay dying, she cursed him and his ancestors. Until one of her own kind willfully took a Hunter to wed, death and destruction on any woman they wed. This was to serve as a warning to the women to stay away from the Hunter men, or so they said." He narrowed his eyes. "One of her brothers made the bell to signify the truth of her curse. This was so long ago that no one even remembers."

Reed stared at him in disbelief. "Do you not see the parallels here? You're a priest, this ancestor who caused all this was also a priest."

"Of course I see," Malcolm snarled. "That's why I alone am fated to be the one who can end the curse. I tried to do this twenty-two years ago. But Brie's mother chose to let our family continue to suffer rather than wed me."

"So you killed her."

"I had to kill her—she was going to go to the bishop

and report me. And how easily they all believed she'd taken her own life. Beautiful Elizabeth Beswick, dead by her own hand."

"Why did you kill Scott Wells? And where's Eldon Brashear?"

Grinning, Malcolm caressed the trigger with his finger. "Often it's necessary for someone to act as sacrifice, in order to set the proper wheels in motion. Eldon played right into my hands, with his undying obsession with Brie's mother. Scott was a bit more difficult. Every time I snuck onto his land, he took potshots at me." He chuckled. "But they're both dead now, so no matter. Like you will soon be, Reed. Why'd you have to get in my way?"

"If you shoot me, you'll be ending our bloodline." There was still a slim chance the other man would listen to reason.

"So be it." Malcolm blinked. In his eyes, Reed saw madness and despair. "If I cannot end the curse, our bloodline deserves to die out."

A cream-colored blur launched itself from the trees.

Malcolm pulled the trigger

The shot went wide.

And Brie, as wolf, ripped out the priest's throat.

Reed leaped forward, shouting her name. Then, while the unconscious Malcolm's throat slowly began to heal, he cuffed him and radioed for backup.

When he looked up again, Brie had gone.

Later, when the state police had taken custody of his uncle, she emerged from the woods, human again. Her hair was wet; evidently she'd found a stream and bathed in it.

Soundlessly, she crossed to his side and watched as the patrol cars and ambulance pulled out, raising dust clouds as they drove away down the dirt road.

"Was he—?" She wouldn't look at him.

"He healed. By the time the paramedics got here, there was only a little cut and a lot of blood."

She grimaced. "I'm glad I didn't kill him." Her fine-boned features wore an expression of shame. "He had silver bullets in his gun. When I heard him say he was going to kill you, I just reacted."

"A she-wolf, protecting her mate."

Her gaze flew to his, bright and startlingly blue. "I never thought I'd hear you say those words. I've always felt we were mates, ever since I changed. But you…" her voice broke. "How long have you known?"

He gathered her in his arms, holding her close to his chest, letting her feel the slow, steady beat of his heart. "Since the first time I heard your thoughts in my head as if they were my own."

She was shaking, though his touch seemed to soothe her. He held her close, murmuring endearments into her hair. Then, to prove the truth of his words, he lifted her chin and kissed her.

"I love you, Brie Danzinger. You are my forever mate, as I am yours. The curse," he swallowed, marveling that the hated words no longer had power over him, "will be no more, if you agree to become my wife, according to my uncle Malcolm."

"Marry you?" Her eyes filled with tears, and for one awful, heart-stopping moment he was afraid she'd refuse. Some of his fear must have shown on his face, for she shook her head. "Can't you hear my thoughts? Try. Listen." And she stood stock still, gazing at him with her gorgeous eyes, full of love.

"Of course I'll marry you." He blinked, drowning in the overwhelming sensation of her feelings. He repeated the words to her, wanting to hear her confirm them, needing to hear her say them out loud.

She smiled and kissed him. "How could you doubt me? Of course I'll marry you, beloved man."

He kissed her again to seal the bargain. Then, when they both came up for air, he smiled. "Let's go over to the church and find that book my uncle talked about. I want to make sure there are no other tasks we must complete before we marry."

"Besides breaking the bell?"

"The bell has to be broken after the vows are said."

Before he'd finished speaking, she shook her head. "Not this time. This time, we're going to try breaking it first, if you're willing."

Hounds, how he loved this woman. "I'm willing."

She leaned close, eyes solemn and twinkling, sorrow mingling with pain on her heart-shaped face. "I wish Malcolm—" Clearing her throat she tried again. "I know one other thing we need to do. We've got to find another priest to marry us. And maybe we can even get him to waive those counseling classes the Church requires."

He kissed her again, wanting to banish the grief from her eyes. "I'll try to talk the priest into it. The sooner we're married, the better."

Two weeks later

With her aunt and uncle flanking them, Reed and Brie entered the church. When they came to the locked door, Reed produced a set of keys and unlocked it.

Eyes bright, Brie gave her aunt a hug and kiss, then

her uncle too. Stepping away, she lifted her chin and looked at Reed.

His dark gaze was solemn. "Are you ready?"

"No fear." As she said the words, she realized for the first time, they were completely true. Her panic attacks had vanished, and she had a feeling they were gone for good.

Uncle Albert looked at Reed. "Are you one hundred percent certain you can break the bell this time? You've tried before and failed."

"I tried alone before," Reed answered. "This time, we both will pull the cord."

"The bell will break." Squeezing Reed's hand, Brie was pleased to see her aunt nodding. "I'm a Beswick, willingly marrying a Hunter. The curse has ended. The time has come."

Reed opened the door that led up to the bell chamber. "Let's go."

"Why are you going all the way up there?" Aunt Marilyn fretted. "If you ring the thing up there, you'll be putting yourselves in danger. The sound alone might kill you, not to mention the vibrations! All you need to do is pull the rope from the ringing chamber down here. There's no need to—"

Reed interrupted her. "For hundreds of years, this bell has resonated with the sound of my family's shame. I want to look at it one final time before it's destroyed."

Their footsteps sounding heavy on the wooden stairs, they climbed the winding staircase to the bell tower. Skirting the cage and wheels carefully, they went to the stone edge at the summit, where the bell could be seen from the street. When they looked out, they discovered crowds had gathered below, in anticipation. Despite the swirling breeze and the overcast sky, which promised rain, the people waited with upturned, hopeful faces.

"That looks like most of the town," Brie said in awe. "What are they doing here?"

"Another tradition. Whenever a Hunter tries to ring the bell and break it and the curse, all of Leaning Tree turns out to bear witness."

"They're not making any noise." Rather than an atmosphere of gaiety, the crowd's mood seemed somber. As a group, they were unbelievably quiet. "Like they're waiting for church to start," she whispered, shivering a little.

"They don't believe I can do it," Reed said. "The curse has remained unbroken in their lifetime and their father's father's lifetime."

She turned to look at him, reached out to touch his beloved face. He stared at the brass monstrosity, an enigmatic expression on his face.

"I, Brie Danzinger, a Beswick, agree willingly to take you, Reed Hunter, as my lawfully wedded husband." As she spoke the words, her eyes filled with tears. "I love you, Reed."

He gazed back, his own face transformed by love. "And I love you, Brie Beswick-Danzinger. Now and for all time."

Above, the roiling clouds parted. A shaft of random sunlight struck the bell, glancing off the dull brass, somehow causing a shimmer so bright she had to close her eyes.

When she opened them again, the sun had gone. Reed still studied the bell, as though he hadn't noticed the spark.

Perhaps it had only been in her mind.

"It's beautiful," he said. Such sorrow and longing vibrated in his voice, making Brie reach out to him.

Reed lifted his head to look at her. His expression was stark, yet his love for her blazed through. "It's time."

They clattered back down to the ground floor, to the ringing chamber. Her aunt and uncle waited solemnly, ready to bear witness.

The thick, ancient rope hung in the middle of the room.

Reed reached for it. "Take hold, Brie. We'll pull it together."

She took the rope in her right hand, reaching out to him with her left. Threading his fingers through hers, he held on.

"One, two, three."

They pulled, hard.

The gears rotated. The bell swung, the clapper struck. The first peal rang out. Clarion. Loud. Reverberating so strongly the entire small room trembled.

When the downward arc of the bell carried it back the other direction, the clapper struck again. Hard. This time, there was only a dull thwack, a hollow sort of ring that carried no weight, no weight at all.

A broken sound, signaling the end of an era.

The end of the curse.

Leaving the rope still twisting, they tore back up to the bell tower, where the massive brass instrument still swung.

"Look!" Brie pointed.

A huge split had appeared in the side of the bell.

As they watched, the crack spread along the entire metal edge, cleaving the brass in two as if by a giant sledgehammer.

Shuddering to a halt, the bell thudded dully. It would ring no more.

Outside, noise from the ground swelled up, low at first, gradually rising in a crescendo of celebratory joy.

"The bell is broken! The curse is gone!"

Reed pulled her into his arms. When he kissed her, the salt of her own tears mingled with his.

"The curse has finally been broken." He spoke against her lips. "My mate, my love."

She smiled, full of love and joy, kissing him back. "Now and forever, we are mates."

And the bell, unnoticed behind them, vanished.

* * * * *

Be sure to read Karen Whiddon's next
Intimate Moments,
THE PRINCESS'S SECRET SCANDAL
Available May 2006 at your favorite retail outlet.

If you enjoyed what you just read,
then we've got an offer you can't resist!

Take 2 bestselling love stories FREE!

Plus get a FREE surprise gift!

Clip this page and mail it to Silhouette Reader Service™

IN U.S.A.	IN CANADA
3010 Walden Ave.	P.O. Box 609
P.O. Box 1867	Fort Erie, Ontario
Buffalo, N.Y. 14240-1867	L2A 5X3

YES! Please send me 2 free Silhouette Intimate Moments® novels and my free surprise gift. After receiving them, if I don't wish to receive anymore, I can return the shipping statement marked cancel. If I don't cancel, I will receive 4 brand-new novels every month, before they're available in stores! In the U.S.A., bill me at the bargain price of $4.24 plus 25¢ shipping and handling per book and applicable sales tax, if any*. In Canada, bill me at the bargain price of $4.99 plus 25¢ shipping and handling per book and applicable taxes**. That's the complete price and a savings of at least 10% off the cover prices—what a great deal! I understand that accepting the 2 free books and gift places me under no obligation ever to buy any books. I can always return a shipment and cancel at any time. Even if I never buy another book from Silhouette, the 2 free books and gift are mine to keep forever.

240 SDN D7ZD
340 SDN D7ZP

Name	(PLEASE PRINT)	
Address	Apt.#	
City	State/Prov.	Zip/Postal Code

Not valid to current Silhouette Intimate Moments® subscribers.

Want to try two free books from another series?
Call 1-800-873-8635 or visit www.morefreebooks.com.

* Terms and prices subject to change without notice. Sales tax applicable in N.Y.
** Canadian residents will be charged applicable provincial taxes and GST.
All orders subject to approval. Offer limited to one per household.
® and ™ are trademarks owned and used by the trademark owner and/or its licensee.

INMOM05   ©2005 Harlequin Enterprises Limited

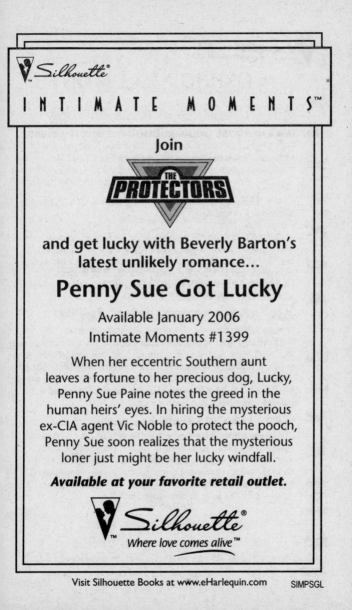